ONE SHOT

BLACK STALLION STUDIOS BOOK 1

VICKI THARP

JPC PUBLISHING

Original Cover Design by Designs EE

ISBN 978-1-948798-17-4

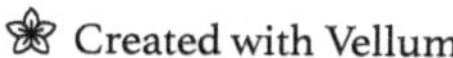 Created with Vellum

ONE SHOT

1

———

ONE MORE PITCH. THAT'S ALL ALEXANDER PAYNE HAD TO MAKE. Bases were loaded. Two outs. Full count. Everything rode on his next pitch.

His dreams.

His career.

His life.

No, it wasn't the bottom of the ninth in game seven of the World Series at Fenway. It was a simulated live inning the day before his Double-A team's last game of the season. And his last chance to prove to his coach—and to the powers that be—that the Tommy John surgery and Alex's struggle through two slow, grinding years of physical therapy and pitching rehab weren't a complete waste of the team's money and faith.

Alex stepped back up to the mound. The stadium seats at Fink Field lay empty except for the few men who held his career in their calloused hands. He dug his toe into the red dirt in front of the rubber and waited for the sign from his catcher.

Curveball.

Fuck. That couldn't be right. Alex removed his cap and wiped the sweat off his brow. He shook his catcher off. Sixty feet and six inches away, Ethan Locke slapped his hand into his catcher's glove and laid down the signs again.

Curveball.

No fucking way. Alex shook Ethan off again.

Locke called time and jogged out to the mound. Alex met him part way. "You *trying* to get me released?" Alex hissed between clenched teeth.

None of the infielders came in. They knew this moment was between him and Locke.

"That kid's already fouled off five pitches. I don't care how fast your fastball is, you throw that pitch within a mile of the strike zone, and that kid's taking you yard. Trust me on this, the curve is his Achilles' heel."

The stack of men on the bases behind Alex proved that a pitcher, even one who could graze a hundred miles per hour, couldn't live by fastball alone.

"My control—"

"Fuck control. Don't get all up in your head. Throw that pitch like you did in your bullpen sessions this week, and the big boys will be dying to re-sign you. Hell, throw it in the dirt if you have to. I'll block it. Trust me. I've got your back, man."

"Yeah." Alex nodded, trying to psych himself up. "You're right. The boy's gonna whiff."

"Damn straight." Locke slapped Alex on the ass with the backside of his glove. "He's going to swing right over it. Just don't leave the ball hanging."

As Locke trotted back to home plate, the cool autumn breeze blew off the San Gabriel Mountains evaporating some of the sweat sticking Alex's jersey to his chest. Locke squatted behind home plate, and Alex carefully placed his foot against the rubber again.

He started from the stretch, looking toward the runner at first base. With the bases loaded, the runner wasn't going anywhere, but Alex took that moment to shift his attention to Coach King in the dugout behind first base. Alex noted the worry on King's face, on the way he chewed at his thumbnail.

King stood at the rail, clapping his hands. "Let's go, kid. Show them what you've got."

Alex refocused on Locke's glove, low and inside. Locke nodded, and in Alex's head, Lock said, "You've got this."

Fuck yeah, he did.

Alex took a deep breath, adjusted his grip on the ball, reared back, and let the ball fly.

———

EVERY MUSCLE IN ELIJAH MADDOX'S BODY SCREAMED FOR RELEASE. The long pose he'd held for almost twenty minutes made his arms ache, his legs quake, and his brain call him seven kinds of fool. But it had been the last pose of the day, so he'd pushed himself.

But that static pose, with his arm out, his leg back as if shooting a bow and arrow had been a nude model's rookie mistake. One he wouldn't ever make again. He breathed through his nose and out through his mouth as the lactic acid built to excruciating levels. The plain institutional clock at the back of Winston College's art studio ticked, the second hand sweeping by the numbers in painstakingly, soul-suckingly, slow motion.

Sweat formed on his brow, and the frigid air from the overhead vent cooled it but did nothing to alleviate his pain.

His eyes drifted down to the art student in front of him. This class he posed for was a sophomore level art class, though the girl—woman really—looked old enough to be in grad school. Sweet, though. The kind of woman he would have wanted waiting for him back home when he'd left for boot camp straight out of high school.

But he'd learned a lot about himself in the eight or nine years since. Some things, it seemed, he continued to learn.

Feeling his eyes on her, her gaze shifted from his crotch and lifted up, up, up to meet his gaze on the dais. Her cheeks flamed, and her hand went to her mouth to cover her giggle as class time ran out. She was beautiful. With big, blue eyes, and long blond hair, and the rocking body all the women in California seemed bound and determined to possess. Despite standing on a stage in front of thirty art students, she should have made him hard.

She didn't.

What the fuck was wrong with him?

She gathered her things, her cheeks aflame, her gaze conspicuously averted as he shrugged into his robe. But instead of scooting out the door as he'd suspected she would, she waited for the room to clear. She approached him as he retrieved his clothes from behind the screen near the back of the room.

"Hey," she said, her voice somehow both timid and brave at the same time. "I don't have another class for an hour. You maybe want to catch a coffee with me at the student center?"

At the back of the room, the professor, Demetri Stavros, stood and came around the front of his desk. He leaned against the front, his arms crossed, not even attempting to hide his interest in their conversation.

The part of Elijah that should have wanted to say yes to the woman, hesitated. The other part of him, that part of him that he'd suppressed even after Uncle Sam repealed Don't Ask, Don't Tell, the *bi* part of him, hitched a thumb towards the door and inanely said, "I've got a thing."

Which totally sounded like he had nothing.

Which he was true.

The way Stavros stared at him from across the room, it made Elijah glad the robe hid that zing of arousal that skittered down his spine and sat heavy in his balls.

"Yeah, sure, I—" She hitched her thumb toward the door the same way he had. "I'll see you next week, then."

"Next week."

He watched her leave. Telling himself to speak up, to stop her, but then she was around the corner, the door closing behind her, and it was too late.

"Pretty woman," Stavros said from beside him. Elijah startled. Did the man not make sounds when he moved? Elijah's training officer would have loved it if Elijah had been able to move with that kind of stealth, but when you were as big as Elijah was, stealth wasn't really in the cards.

Then again, if you were looking for a bull-in-a-china-shop kind of guy, Elijah was your man.

"If you say so, Mr. Stavros." Elijah reached for his underwear, not bothering to change behind the screen.

If the military taught him one thing, it was that there was little room in his life for false modesty. Besides, you didn't do work as a live model if you cared if someone saw you naked.

"Demetri. Call me Demetri."

"Demetri it is then."

Demetri waited until Elijah had pulled his jeans on and discarded the robe before pulling a business card out of his back pocket. Elijah pulled his ITMFA T-shirt over his head and reached for the card. "What's this?"

Demetri held on to the other end. "My personal contact information. I have my own art studio at my house. You need extra money... call me. I pay triple the college's hourly rate. I'm always looking for new, interesting subjects to model for me." Then he released the card. "Among other things."

The professor's voice had dropped, rippling goosebumps along Elijah's skin.

Among other things.

"I'm not sure how to respond to that."

"No, is an acceptable answer. It won't affect your work here. You have my word on that."

Elijah stared at the card, it had Demetri's name and phone number. Nothing else. Was Demetri looking for a model or a bit on the side? Or both? Elijah wasn't sure if he should be unsettled or tempted. "And the 'among other things'?"

Demetri tugged at the half-inch gauge in his right ear. He had tattoos creeping up past the collar of his dark-blue, button-up shirt and peeking out beneath the sleeves he'd rolled partway up his forearms.

He looked like the Mediterranean version of a typical California skater kid who'd aged out of the sport. Not that Demetri had allowed himself to go to pot. For a guy Elijah pegged at being in his mid-forties, he kept himself in decent, lean-muscled, skater-dude shape.

Demetri shrugged, a loose-limbed, no-skin-off-my-back kind of motion. "You..." The professor looked Elijah up and down, his gaze snagging on the tight bulge in Elijah's jeans on the way up. "...intrigue me. I'd like a chance to get to know you better."

The extra modeling work would be a boon to his cash flow issue, or should Elijah say, his lack of cash flow issue, but it was the personal interest beneath the job offer that Elijah would have to think about. One of the things he'd learned about his bi side, was that while he'd found himself attracted to men, he didn't want a romantic relationship with one.

And Demetri had long-term, till-death-do-us-part kind of guy written all over his face. As much as Elijah needed the money, he didn't need the personal entanglement. He had classes to get through, an engineering degree to finish, and a whole new, post military life to start.

Elijah pocketed the card. "Thanks, I'll keep the offer in mind."

After stuffing the robe into his backpack, Elijah headed for the door. Demetri's voice reached him as he grabbed the door-knob. "You're not going to call, are you?"

Elijah turned and decided to be direct. "I've only ever been with women."

Demetri noticed what he *didn't* say. "That's not the same thing as saying you're straight."

"I think it's better this way."

"Even though you need the money."

"Maybe especially because I need the money."

Demetri stared at him. Not in an aggressive, put out kind of way, but in that quiet, thoughtful, professor kind of way. "Fuck," Demetri muttered and pulled a different business card out of his wallet.

The silver embossed letters on a glossy black background said *Black Stallion Studios*, the name underneath read *Niko Stavros* followed by a phone number.

"That's my cousin. He can help you with your cash situation," Demetri said. "Tell him I sent you."

***

BACK AT HIS APARTMENT, ALEX LAY SPRAWLED ON HIS COUCH while listening to the Los Angeles Grizzlies baseball game playing on his laptop on the coffee table.

The Los Angeles Grizzlies.

The Major League team he would never play for again. He'd had his moment in the spotlight. That day all kids dreamed about. The one where they take the field in the big leagues.

Except that one day, Alex's *best* day, had also been his last, and his worst. Thanks to the ligament in his elbow that tore clear through.

Which, two years later, accounted for why his computer lay buried amongst the empty beer cans, the crusty pizza boxes, and the crumpled chip bags. His stomach bitched and complained and threatened a revolt, but Alex refused to vomit and let his abused stomach win.

He threw an arm over his eyes. His stomach churned, and the bile rose up the back of his throat. Groaning, he swallowed the bitter taste. Someone pounded on his door. Not someone. *Trevor Moon.* Alex's physical therapist since his surgery. Alex knew it was him because no one else really cared enough to come knocking.

"Go away," Alex hollered out.

"Open the damn door."

Fuck that.

Trevor pounded on the door again, but Alex just rolled over and covered his ears with a pillow. If he ignored Trevor long enough, he'd go away.

Alex had no idea how long it took Trevor to give up, but he finally did. *Thank fucking Christ.* The tinny voice of the announcer droned on and on as the baseball game went into extra innings. Alex shouldn't have been listening. Listening and watching the games now was like grinding gun powder into an open wound and lighting it on fire to see how much it hurt.

The two-word answer: A fuck-ton.

Having the elbow surgery sans anesthesia would have been less painful. At least maybe then he could pass out from the pain like they did in all those westerns Hollywood had spit out back in the day.

But as much as Alex had tried to drink himself into oblivion, the masochistic part of him wouldn't let him *not* feel the pain of his dying career.

The deadbolt turned in his door, and Trevor and the apartment's maintenance guy stumbled in. Alex rolled over. His stomach did, too. Before he could yell for the intruders to get lost, he heaved and heaved. The vomit hit the cheap linoleum with a wet, slapping sound. The stench of sour beer and fermented pepperoni burned the hair in his nose.

"*Jesus*," the maintenance man said. "I ain't cleaning that up."

"I've got it," Trevor said. "Thanks for letting me in."

"You best get this hell hole cleaned up, or I'm calling the manager."

Alex spat the foul taste out of his mouth while Trevor pushed the man out the door.

"*Dude.*" Trevor approached the couch, his shirt collar pulled up over his nose and mouth. "What the hell is up with you?"

Alex lifted the arm covering his eyes long enough to glare at Trevor. "Like you don't know."

"So, the Hawks let you go. Curveballs hang. It's not the end of the world."

Alex didn't have the energy to glare again. "Fuck you."

"You're not my type."

Alex chuckled, half-hearted and morose. "If they've got a dick, they're your type."

"Not the closet cases. They're not worth the trouble."

"And it's called straight. I'm not in the closet."

"Yeah, keep telling yourself that, buddy."

Trevor tossed Alex's sweatpants over his crotch and said, "And get some damn clothes on."

"I've got clothes on."

"No, you have compression shorts on, and all the stains tell me you haven't changed or showered since Coach King had to drop you from the team."

Alex sat up and tugged on his sweatpants, though he didn't see the point. They spent the next twenty minutes cleaning up the puke—which almost made Alex puke again—and sweeping the piles of trash and take-out containers into a trash bag.

When they'd finished, Alex plopped back on the couch,

staring at the baseball game, but not really watching. It hurt too damn much.

Trevor slapped his hand down on the laptop's lid, and the room went silent.

"What the hell did you do that for?"

Instead of answering, Trevor sat on the coffee table across from him and said, "You've missed three PT sessions already. You haven't thrown a baseball in a week. You've had time to wallow, now it's time to get your ass sober and back to work."

"It's over, Trev. Let me be."

"Bullshit. Maybe you didn't heal on their timeline, but you're so damn close. Your dream isn't over. You were the number fucking one draft pick for a reason. No one has forgotten that. You work hard, maybe you can finagle an invite to spring training."

Alex scrubbed a hand down his face, a week's worth of scruff scratching against his palm. "What part of 'being released' do you not understand?"

"The part where you fucking give up. That's not the Alexander Payne I know." Trevor stood and held out his hand.

"What?"

"Come on. You're hitting the showers, and then we're hitting the gym."

"I'm a free agent. The league isn't footing your bills anymore. I'm already a month behind on my lease, I can't afford—"

"I can float my fees for you for a week, maybe two, before my boss catches on."

"Then what? I'm not gonna make the kind of money I need flipping burgers."

Trevor got this grin, this calculating, mischievous, gorgeous grin—and just because Trevor had a great smile, and just because Alex noticed, didn't mean anything. Right? "I know where you can get a pile of cash fast."

"I'm not selling drugs."

Trevor rolled his eyes. "You've got something even better to sell. Scoot over."

Alex would have asked what Trevor had up his sleeve, but a guy like Trevor, with a bodybuilder physique, didn't wear shirts with sleeves, he wore those low-cut tanks with the thin straps that showed off every muscle he'd been perfecting over the last ten years.

Though skeptical of Trevor's idea, Alex scooted over. Trevor pulled the computer onto his lap and typed *Black Stallion Studios* into the search engine.

Alex laughed. "You want me to make porn?"

"Not just any porn. *Gay* porn."

"I'm straight."

"So you keep saying. And because of that, they pay a hell of a lot more than what the other studios pay."

2

IT WAS LATE ON A FRIDAY AFTERNOON WHEN THE MAP ON ELIJAH'S phone directed him to turn right into his destination. Ahead, Black Stallion Studios' wrought iron gate stood open, and he pulled through. The thick bars and exaggerated height made it look like something built to keep a Tyrannosaurus Rex from escaping, not something to keep prying eyes at bay.

He followed the winding, well-landscaped road to the covered porte-cochere per the instruction on his acceptance email. The building he pulled up to had two wings, both boxy, with hard lines, cantilevered terraces, and miles of glass. Something a Frank Lloyd Wright wanna-be might have designed.

From the information Black Stallion had given him, one wing belonged to Black Stallion's owner and director, Niko Stavros. The other one housed the men for the shoots. Elijah didn't know what to expect for the weekend, hell, he didn't even know if he wanted to be there. He'd made his rent for the month, barely, but his truck payment was almost due, and he'd spent his last twenty bucks on gas driving to the studios.

Elijah turned off the engine but didn't make a move to leave his truck.

It's only a jack-off scene. Might as well get paid for something you already do.

Except he usually didn't do it in front of cameras and a bunch of strangers.

How is that different than live modeling?

He wasn't sure. But it was. The most unsettling thing? The idea of being filmed until he made himself come, kinda turned him on.

But...

Fuck it.

He could find another way to make a few bucks. He had Demetri's card. He shoved his keys back into the ignition as knuckles rapped on his driver's side window.

Elijah buzzed the window down. The guy at the window put his hands on the sill and leaned down. "Don't tell me you're chickening out, dude."

Elijah laughed. "You here for a shoot?"

"Yeah. First time." The man held out his hand. He had sun-bleached hair that curled up at his collar and one of those long, lean bodies you'd expect from an elite athlete. But then again, this was Southern California, almost every other guy looked like him. Or wanted to. "Alex Payne."

"Elijah Maddox." They shook, the contact lasting a beat too long. Had that been on his end or Alex's? "It's my first time, too."

Alex popped Elijah's door and held it open. "Come on, fellow porn virgin. Don't make me go in there alone."

At Elijah's hesitation, Alex made the *bock bock* chicken noise, though the grin on his face made Elijah chuckle. "Not sure if it's a chicken thing as much as a fork-in-the-road kind of thing. You know, the fork where one path has all the twists and turns and pitfalls and the other is nothing but clear skies and a carefree hike."

"I hear ya." Alex leaned an arm on top of the open door.

"The only trouble is, you don't know which path you're on until it's too late to turn back."

"Tell me about it."

"And I'm betting neither one of us would be here if we didn't need the money. Am I right?"

Fuuuck. Elijah pressed the release button on his seatbelt.

Alex clapped Elijah on the shoulder as he climbed out. "Good man. Let's get checked in and see what the fuss is all about."

They were led into a long hallway outside Niko Stavros' office and told to wait there for their turn to sign their contracts. Already, three men were waiting in chairs lining a wall decorated with photographs from porn shoots.

The photographs ranged the whole spectrum from modern to old-timey. From a vanilla handjob to leather and chains and gang bangs. All tastefully matted, framed, and hung as if they graced the walls of a modern art museum.

The men introduced themselves around. A tall, muscular black man was the first to stick out his hand. "Darius Williams. They pay me to bring the D," he said, straight-faced and cocky.

"You wish," a short, stocky Hispanic man beside Darius said. "If anyone is paid to bring the D, it's Hardy."

"You two the fresh ass they've promised us?" Darius asked.

"Uhhh... Umm...," Alex stammered. "I'm here—"

The Hispanic man jammed his elbow in Darius' ribs. "Fuck, man, you're gonna scare the young pups off."

Darius burst out laughing, his smile expanded from ear to ear. "I'm messing with you fools."

The guy with the elbow said, "I'm Reynaldo Reyes." Then he hitched a thumb at a guy sitting at the end, his nose in a book. "That's the old man. Grant Hardy."

"Old man, my ass." The guy never glanced up from his book.

Grant couldn't have been more than a few years older than

Elijah, early thirties at the most, but Elijah figured youth had its advantages in the porn industry.

"Don't mind him," Darius said, "he's trying to finish his book. He doesn't know how Snow White ends."

"Spoiler alert," Reyes said, "no one gets fucked in the ass."

"Not unless you read that erotic version," Darius piped in. "Where those dwarfs—"

A door opened, and a middle-aged woman with graying hair stuck her head out. "We're ready for you, Grant."

Grant wedged a bookmark between the pages and left the book on the chair. He greeted the woman with a hug and a kiss on the cheek. "How's my favorite person?"

The woman rolled her eyes. "If you're trying to get on my good side so I'll schedule you for the early shoot, you're wasting your breath. You know we shoot all the easy stuff first."

"Damn."

Then to the rest of them—but mostly to Reyes and Darius from the looks she gave them—the woman asked, "You boys behaving?"

Grant snorted. "You're kidding me, right?"

"Aw, Ms. Rose, you know there ain't no fun in that," Darius gave her a big, cheesy smile.

Grant disappeared through the door. Before Rose left, she mouthed the words 'behave,' though the smile she fought cut the sting.

"Have a seat, my man." Reyes picked Grant's thick tomb of a book off the chair. Reyes read the title out loud, "*Guns, Germs, and Steel.*" Then dropped it on the floor at his feet.

"Christ," Elijah said, "the foundation shuddered."

"Gives a whole new meaning to *heavy* reading," Alex deadpanned, finally finding more of his voice.

Alex had been the one who'd talked Elijah into staying, now the guy looked like he was two seconds away from bolting.

Elijah pointed to the vacated chair and to Alex said, "Go ahead."

"Thanks," Alex muttered as he brushed past Elijah.

At least this way Alex would have to go through him if the guy decided to go AWOL.

"Hey, man," Reyes said to Alex, "Don't I know you from somewhere?"

The color drained from Alex's face. "No, man. I've got one of those faces, you know?"

Elijah eyed Alex. Come to think of it...

"Naw, man." Darius shook his finger at Alex as if trying to place where he'd seen him before. "Reyes is right. You look familiar. *Really* familiar."

Reyes snapped his fingers. "You ever do straight porn?"

Alex shook his head.

"Look at that face, man." Darius wouldn't let it drop. "He's got one of them innocent faces. It's the innocent looking ones who are the kinkiest. I'll bet Reyes' left nut—"

"Hey," Reyes hollered in protest. "Bet your own damn nuts."

"Fine, you wuss," Darius said, glancing at the heavens or the gaudy crystal chandelier hanging high above. Were those...? Were those penis-shaped cut crystal pieces hanging from the lights? "I'll bet *my* left nut that you've done one of those pup play vids—"

"Definitely not," Alex said.

Reyes snapped his fingers again. "You're a furry. You were in *Furry Fitness* and *The Fast and the Furriest*—"

"What the fuck is a furry?" Alex asked Elijah.

Elijah shrugged. Who the fuck knew?

Reyes and Darius lapsed into silence, but the wheels churned in their heads as they tried to place where they knew Alex from.

The door opened and spat Grant out. He kicked Reyes' foot

off his book and picked it up, his eyes narrowing when he got a good look at Alex. "Hey, man, don't I know you from somewhere?"

Alex glanced up at Elijah, his expression screaming *help me*. But before Elijah could say anything, Darius was called into the office, and Grant left to get his gear from his vehicle.

Elijah took Darius' seat, a knot of concern tightening in the pit of his stomach. He could still say no until he signed on the bottom line, until the cameras started to roll. It wasn't too late.

It didn't take long for Darius and Reyes to finish their contracts and for Rose to call out to Elijah and Alex. "Niko is ready for you boys. He wants to talk to you together since you're both new."

Elijah glanced over at Alex. He had the most adorable here-goes-nothing curve to his lips. *Adorable?* Where the hell had that come from?

Talk about getting into character for a part.

And he guessed if there was a time to appreciate his bi side, it was right before shooting a scene with Black Stallion. Being housed with a group of hot, sexy guys certainly wasn't a draw-back to the gig.

But to say his stomach hadn't developed a nauseating twist considering what he was about to sign up for, would be a lie.

What the hell are you doing?

"Yo, bro," Alex said from the doorway to Niko's office. Darius and Reyes had both disappeared, presumably to get their stuff out of their vehicles as well. "You coming?"

It wasn't like he had to make a career in front of the camera. He just needed to get out of his financial bind. As soon as he got that monkey off his back, he'd quit. If his mother could see him now... scratch that. She definitely wouldn't want to see *that*.

Elijah stood. "Yeah, I'm coming."

In more ways than one.

———

ALEX DIDN'T KNOW WHAT HE'D EXPECTED THE OFFICE OF ONE OF the top gay porn directors and producers to look like. But the enormity of the room shouldn't have been a surprise considering the sheer size of the building and the popularity that Black Stallion Studios appeared to enjoy online.

Inside, the decorating theme from the hallway carried through to the office with stylized photos from porn shoots, both vintage and from recent years. On the wall opposite a bookcase, was a glass case displaying a vast collection of sex toys. From dildos and vibrators of every shape and size, to floggers, gags, and leather restraints.

"Interesting collection, Mr. Stavros." Alex reached out to shake the director's hand. "Beats my grandmother's collection of Hummel figurines."

Stavros chuckled, his voice deep, his smile genuine. "Call me Niko."

Niko had one of those ageless, olive-skinned, Mediterranean looks. Not the typical Californian Botox-induced kind, but the works-hard-to-stay-fit kind. He had fine lines radiating from the corners of his eyes and flecks of gray in his dark hair at his temples and peppered throughout his manicured beard.

But Alex had done his research. Niko was in his mid-forties, a porn star in his own right back in his early days. In impressive shape, he could probably strip naked and put a lot of his performers to shame.

Alex made a mental note to get the name of Niko's personal trainer, in case his thing with Trevor fell through.

After shaking Elijah's hand, Niko said, "You boys have a seat."

Instead of walking behind a sleek glass desk tall enough and wide enough to be perfect for fucking, Niko ushered them through to a seating area overlooking a pool and patio. Alex and Elijah sat on the black leather sofa with clean, chrome lines, while Niko settled into a matching leather chair across from them.

Rose came in and laid a couple of manila folders on the coffee table. To him and Elijah she said, "When you two are finished here, bring your things into the other wing, and I'll get you settled in. I've got the two of you sharing a room since Niko has you in a scene together. I figured it would give you a chance to get to know each other better first."

"Excuse me?" Elijah croaked.

"A scene? Together?" Alex asked. "I thought—"

Rose's gaze snapped to Niko's. "Sorry, did I miss something?"

"It's fine, Rose." If Niko was annoyed, Alex couldn't detect it in his voice or see it in his demeanor. "Why don't you check on the others. I'll go over the contracts."

Elijah waited for Rose to leave before he turned to Niko. "I thought we'd agreed on a solo—"

Niko silenced Elijah's objection with a raised hand. He leaned forward, resting his forearms on his knees, his gold chain swinging against the mat of black hair at the top of the open neck of his shirt.

"The solo scenes are in the plans, and they are great for popping your porn cherry, but I think, especially now that I've seen you two together, that a jack-off scene with the two of you would be off the charts."

Elijah glanced at Alex and gave him one of those what-do-you-think faces with a non-committal shrug. Not that any shrug in the history of shrugs had ever been decisive.

To Niko, Alex asked, "What does this mean for our bottom line?" Because really, that's why they were there.

"More money. Significantly. Your pay goes up with what you're willing to do. The two of you jacking-off beside each other is one thing. Add kissing, mutual masturbation, a blow job..."

Niko threw in one of his own shrugs as if he really wasn't heavily invested in what Alex and Elijah would agree to do, but his nonchalance seemed forced.

"And the two of you together... the viewers are going to eat you guys up. Here at Black Stallion, we pay the flat fee for each scene, but we also pay a percentage of downloads. The hotter the scene, the more it gets downloaded, and the more money you two make. Simple."

"Do we have to decide right now?" Elijah's voice went up an octave.

"ASAP so we'll have time to schedule the extra scene."

Someone knocked on the office door but didn't bother to wait for a reply before it opened and a young man walked through. Alex figured the guy couldn't be much younger than himself, but the slight body and boyish features made him look much younger.

"Bass," Niko admonished, "You need to wait."

"You have an important call."

Niko nodded toward Alex and Elijah. "This is my assistant, Sebastian. Sebastian, meet Elijah Maddox and—"

"Alex Payne." Sebastian slapped a hand over his mouth. "Oh my fucking gay God. Alex fucking Payne." Then he squealed like a schoolgirl who'd caught sight of this month's answer to Justin Bieber.

"You'll have to excuse him," Niko said. "He's not normally anything like this."

Elijah grinned. It was the first full smile Alex had seen from him since they'd met and if Alex weren't straight, he would think that dimple that popped out in his cheek was damn adorable. "Darius is going to be mad he lost his left nut in a bet."

Sebastian whipped out a pen from his back pocket and

dropped to his knees in front of Alex. What the actual fuck? Sebastian held out the pen. "Sign my shirt?"

"Someone mind telling me what the hell is going on?" Niko asked.

"If you knew anything about—"

"*Bass.*" Niko gave Alex an apologetic smile. "You'll have to forgive my nephew he's—"

"In love," Sebastian finished for his uncle. "Please say you'll fuck my ass and inseminate me with your baseball babies."

"He can't get you pregnant." Niko snagged Sebastian's sleeve and pulled him to his feet. "I should have known. Bass has a thing for baseball players."

"Won't hurt for him to try though," Sebastian said with a pout. "Miracles happen, and anything is possible if it's gay God's will."

The heat settled in Alex's cheeks and he couldn't think of what to say.

"Why didn't you tell me you were famous?" Niko didn't look pleased, and by the way the crease formed between his brows and the way his biceps bulged when he crossed his arms over his chest, the man looked seriously pissed.

"Um... I'm not famous. There was a chance at one time that I was going to be somebody, but that's behind me now."

"This adds a complication," Niko said. "Have you thought—"

"Uh, Niko." Sebastian cut in. "That call?"

Niko cut his eyes to his nephew. "Who is it?"

Sebastian swallowed hard and took a step back. "Peter." He half-whispered the word as if ready to make a run for it if Niko exploded.

Niko's eyes closed for a beat as he took in a deep breath. "Tell him I'll call him back."

"He says it's urgent."

"With Peter, it's always urgent. As soon as I'm done here—"

Sebastian scrunched up his nose. "He was crying."

"*Fuck.*" Niko stood. "This is why relationships are a bad idea. This should only take a minute."

Sebastian took his pen out of his back pocket again and approached Alex. Niko clapped a hand on the back of his nephew's neck and ushered him toward the door. Before Niko left the room, he turned back and said, "While I'm gone, you two talk about that extra scene."

3

———

Elijah chuckled. "So... Not a furry porn star."

"What just happened here?" Alex looked dazed.

"Pretty sure you got fangirled." Then Elijah looked Alex up and down. Alex was a good half-a-head taller than Elijah, and he was six foot. Alex had to have the wingspan of a bald eagle. "Pitcher?" Elijah guessed.

Alex nodded, the wattage in his eyes dimming like a New York City brownout in the summer.

"What happened?"

Alex tugged the sleeve of his dress shirt up, exposing the four-inch scar on the inside of his right elbow. "Happened during my Major League debut with the Los Angeles Grizzlies two years ago."

"Sorry, dude. That's..." Elijah didn't know what to say. "That's..."

"Fucked up," Alex said. "But it is what it is."

Alex rolled his sleeve back down as if leaving it up left him feeling more exposed. "About that extra scene..."

For the first time, Elijah allowed his gaze to drop to Alex's lips and the scruff of blond stubble surrounding them. He'd always been partial to scruff on a man, and it would be a lie if he said he'd never been curious about wanting to feel the scratch and the scrape of it against his face. "I don't see a problem with us kissing."

"It's not a big deal, right?"

"First base stuff."

"What about...?" Alex made a pumping motion with his closed fist. His hands were huge. His fingers long. He had to have one hell of a grip.

Blood surged south, and Elijah crossed his legs to hide his growing erection. Now wasn't the time to sprout wood. "It's not like we've never had a dick in our hand before. Am I right?"

Alex barked out a laugh as the red crept into his cheeks. "Fuck. No lie, man."

So, they were on the same page with kissing and giving each other a hand job. That left...

"I don't know about the other." Alex shifted on the couch and couldn't meet Elijah's eyes.

Was it wrong that Elijah *did* know how he felt about the proposed blow job?

The thought of Alex's dick in his mouth, all that athletic meat—and don't forget the real reason they were both there: the added money—certainly sweetened a deal that to Elijah's curious bi side already sounded quite tasty.

Elijah cleared his throat. "I could... you know. Go down on you, I guess." Elijah hesitated again. If he sounded too eager the guy might bolt. "If you closed your eyes... you could pretend..."

Alex's eyes lingered on Elijah's mouth for a beat before meeting his gaze and swallowing hard. For a supposedly straight guy, Alex didn't seem *too* freaked out, especially considering he'd come to Black Stallion, the way Elijah had—thinking he'd only be doing a solo scene. Was it Elijah's wishful imagination or did Alex seem... intrigued?

Alex's leg bounced a couple times, then Alex quieted himself with a large hand on his knee. He sat back. "I'm not going to pretend the extra money isn't tempting."

Yeah. Money talked. And in this case, could talk a straight guy into oral sex with another man.

Niko returned, his expression flat except for that valley digging between his brows and the stiff, agitated way he carried himself. He sat on the edge of the leather chair as if he didn't plan on staying long. "What did you two decide?"

"We're going to do the extra scene," Elijah said, not giving Alex the chance to back out. After all, Elijah was there for the money as well. The faster he got caught up on his bills and built a big enough nest egg to get him through the last two semesters of college, the sooner he could put this part of his life behind him.

"Have you thought about what will happen when you get recognized?" Niko asked Alex. "Because it is a *when* not an *if*. Your situation is different than Elijah's. No one cares if Joe Blow does gay porn. You on the other hand... with the paucity of out gay baseball players, you getting outed for being in gay porn could become a real media shit storm. As far as Black Stallion is concerned, we welcome the publicity. For you, it could be more than you bargained for."

"My baseball career is over."

"Still. It's not a decision to make lightly."

"I need the money."

"There are worse things than being broke."

Elijah laughed. "Says the man living in a multi-million-dollar home."

Niko inclined his head with deference, but added, "I didn't always live this way." He didn't elaborate, but Elijah didn't doubt there was a story there.

Alex didn't respond. After a thoughtful minute, Niko said,

"I'll tell you what. We can shoot you from the neck down. It's not my preference, but I think until you've had more of a chance to think about how this could affect your future, it's a compromise we could both live with."

"Sounds like a plan," Alex said.

Then Niko focused on Elijah, "What about you?"

Elijah raised his hands. "I've got nothing to hide."

Leaning forward, Niko opened each of the manila folders. "Your contracts, boys. I'm going to need your paperwork from your STI screening, and this is the general liability release, which also outlines payment for scenes and what to expect from residuals. Pay special attention to line five, what everyone affectionately calls the *Straight Clause.*"

"The Straight Clause?" Elijah asked.

"Basically, you're affirming to Black Stallion Studios that you're straight. We pride ourselves on this. Many other studios will say their performers are straight, we're the only ones who make you put your money where your mouth is."

Alex picked up the contract in front of him and flipped to the enumerated clause in question. "How's that?"

"If we find out that you're gay, not only will you never work for Black Stallion again, you forfeit all rights to your residuals."

Alex glanced at Elijah, then back at Niko. "No problem here."

Niko focused on Elijah. "And you?"

"Same."

They both skimmed through the document and signed on the dotted line. After all, even though Elijah had found himself attracted to men in the past, he'd never kissed a man, much less had sex with one. That means he could effectively round himself up to straight. Right?

———

ALL THE GUYS HAD GATHERED AROUND A LARGE WHITE MARBLE kitchen island by the time Alex and Elijah had dumped their duffel bags in their shared room. Grant stood at the stove, slaving over a boiling pot of water. He poured in a box of noodles and turned the burner down on a bubbling pot of spaghetti sauce.

"Reyes," Grant said, "Stop stuffing your face with chips and dip and set the damn table already. And, Darius, you're on dish duty tonight."

"What the fuck, man?" Darius complained around a mouthful of tortilla chips. "Why do I always have to wash the dishes?"

"Because Reyes made the salsa and you burn water. You learn to cook something other than microwave pizza, I'll be happy to do the dishes for your sorry ass."

"Hell, man, ain't nothin' wrong with zapped pizza, it's—"

"*Boys.*" Rose walked into the kitchen with a moon-eyed, trying-to-hide-the-fangirl Sebastian behind her. Alex was almost afraid to make eye contact and set him off again. "I'm going to go over the house rules."

"House rules?" Alex dug a chip into the salsa. What was this, high school?

"One." Grant stuck a spoon in the sauce and took a taste. "Ms. Rose isn't your mother, so pick up your own shit."

"Two," Reyes added. "Division of house duties is decided *equally* between the performers." That comment seemed aimed more at Grant than anyone else.

Grant stirred in what looked like oregano and muttered, "Someone has to take charge and be the adult around here. Not my fault you guys squabble like spoiled children."

"And the most important rule?" Rose asked the room in general.

Darius grinned a big toothy grin. "No draining the sac."

Elijah choked on a chip.

Reyes clapped Elijah on the back. It didn't seem to help. "He means no jerking off. Gotta save the spunk for the big screen."

Elijah cut Reyes a look that said *get-real*. "I know what 'draining the sac' means."

"Any questions?" Sebastian asked.

Reyes raised his hand. Rose twisted her hair into a bun and stuck her pen through it to hold it in place. "This isn't grade school, Reynaldo, you don't have to raise your hand."

"I wanna know why Grant gets his own room. Is he, like, boning Niko on the side or something, because that's a price I'm willing to pay if I don't have to share a room with Darius again. He watches porn all night. I can't get any sleep."

Darius draped an arm around Reyes' shoulder. "It's called research, asshole. I gotta keep one step ahead of the competition. You think those boys over at *Men on Men* or *PornU* are going to bed early and dreaming of tamales all night? No, they're—"

"Jesus Christ," Grant said. "Would you two quit arguing and fuck each other already?"

Darius plopped a salsa loaded chip into his mouth. Around the bite of food, he said, "I would, but I can't violate rule number three. Rose would get the paddle and—"

"Oooh," Reyes said, "Sounds kinky. I'm in. But that doesn't tell me why Grant gets his own room."

"I'll tell you what, Reynaldo," Rose said, "when you're the biggest stud in Black Stallion's stable, you can have your own room, too."

Grant grinned as he poured the cooked noodles into the strainer, the cloud of steam rising and nearly obliterating his face from view. "Time to eat, boys."

"Alex, Elijah," Rose said. "You two shoot first thing in the morning. Be down in the studio by seven. The rest of you guys don't need to show up until around nine."

"We'll be there," Alex said.

Sebastian held back as Rose started to leave. "You coming, Bass?"

"I need Alex to sign one more thing." Sebastian held up a manila folder similar to what had held Alex's contract, but Sebastian's cheeks went red, and he wouldn't meet Rose's eyes.

"*Bass.*" Rose had that motherly what-are-you-up-to tone. She didn't wait for an answer. Instead she strode back over to the island and snatched the folder out of Sebastian's hand. A photograph slipped free and floated to the tile floor. A photograph of Alex in his San Fernando Hawks' uniform from two years ago.

Elijah bent and picked it up and laid it on the counter. Grant, Darius, and Reyes gathered around. Reyes laughed, and to Alex said, "Holy shit, hermano. You *are* somebody."

Alex used to revel on those rare occasions that he'd been recognized on the street. But now, it made him feel like day-old, dried-up crap. "That was a long time ago."

Grant clapped Alex on the back and grabbed the bowl of pasta off the island. "I knew that I knew you from somewhere. Looks like we got ourselves a superstar."

"Hardly," Alex said.

"What's this all about?" Rose asked.

Grant returned to the stove and began ladling the sauce into a bowl.

Elijah laughed, and said, "Sebastian loves him some Alex."

Grant paused, the ladle halfway between the pot and the bowl. His eyes went to Sebastian. After a heartbeat or two, Grant said, "Does he, now?"

Sebastian swallowed hard. "I—"

"I call dibs," Darius said.

"Dibs?" Reyes laughed. "You're loco."

"My wife loves baseball. I tell her I dipped my dick in some baseball ass, she won't let me out of bed for a week. Oh, man, our seventh anniversary is coming up." Darius turned his attention to Alex. "You think maybe I can get your number and you know... You two could..." Darius waggled his brows up and down.

Grant set the bowl with the pasta sauce on the table, with a loud crack. The ceramic didn't shatter, though it should have. "I don't know what you traditionally give as gifts for a seventh anniversary, but I'm pretty sure it isn't dick."

"Well it should be," Sebastian muttered.

"Ain't that the truth," Rose said. "I'm out of here, boys, you all have a nice night."

Darius looked at Alex, waiting for an answer. What was he supposed to say to that proposition? He'd had the occasional baseball bunny chase after him in the Minor Leagues—which he'd taken advantage of a time or two because... hey... sex—but he'd never had a man offer him up as a gift to his wife. "Um..."

"Here's a pen." Sebastian held up the fine-tipped Sharpie.

Alex shoved Darius' offer out of his mind. Surely, he was joking, right? "Yeah, sure, Sebastian."

Alex scribbled his name across the mound at his feet and handed the Hawks' eight by ten promotional glossy back to Sebastian who had that embarrassed, dreamy look in his eyes.

Sebastian took the folder back. "Thanks. I'll let you guys eat before your dinner gets cold. See you in the morning."

They all found a seat around the table. The conversation and ribbing died down and was replaced by more mundane words like "Pass the bread" and "Hey, jerk-wad, I need more sauce than that."

Alex didn't realize he'd been staring until Darius glanced up at him, his mouth half-full of spaghetti noodles. "What?" The word came out muffled.

Alex twirled the noodles around his fork. "You guys really all straight?"

"Ask my girlfriend," Reyes said.

"A hundred percent," Darius said. "I even got two kids. Not that that proves anything or that you've gotta be straight to have kids, but I am and I do."

Grant was slow to answer, but then he swallowed and said, "Those are the rules."

Elijah helped himself to another piece of garlic bread and glanced across the table at Darius. "Your wife knows what you do? And she's okay with it?"

Darius chuckled, his grin wide and his eyes bright. "Oh hell yeah. I was a bricklayer before. You know how much a bricklayer makes?"

"Not a clue," Elijah said.

"A hell of a lot less than a gay porn performer. More money. Less hours. And it's a hell of a lot easier to do the heavy lifting with my dick instead of my back. Besides, those kids, they ain't cheap."

Alex pushed his empty plate back and wiped his mouth. "What about you, Reyes. Your girlfriend know?"

Reyes threw his crumpled napkin on his plate. "No, man. She has no clue. And if she finds out, she'd be gone."

"That sucks." Alex glanced down the table at Grant. The man was awfully quiet.

Reyes shrugged one of those it-is-what-it-is kind of shrugs.

Elijah stacked Alex's empty plate on top of his and reached across the table for Reyes'. "What does your girlfriend think you do for a living? How do you explain your time away for the shoots?"

Reyes smiled, but there were no teeth, and it didn't reach his eyes. "She thinks I run drugs over the border."

Darius barked out a laugh. "Your old lady thinks you're a mule? And that's better than finding out you do gay porn?"

"She doesn't *know* know. But she suspects. And I let her."

"That's a fucked-up way to run a relationship." Grant was

proving to be a man of few words, but apparently couldn't hold back his opinion.

"At least I have a relationship," Reynaldo spat back, with a touch of heat thrown in for the first time. "Her family is very religious. They don't believe in gays."

"Don't 'believe in gays'." Grant slammed his glass of water on the table. "For fuck's sake. What do you think they would say if they knew their little girl's boyfriend supported her with the money he made from all the gays who watch porn? Do you think they would believe then?"

Grant stomped off to the kitchen and dumped the dirty pots and pans into the sink. "I'm going to bed. I've had enough."

Alex waited for Grant to disappear behind his closed door before he said to Reyes and Darius, "Sorry, guys, I didn't mean—"

"Naw, man. It's all good." Darius cleared the food from the table. "I don't know what's up with Grant, but he's had a bug up his ass for a while now."

4

AFTER HIS SHOWER, ELIJAH SLIPPED ON A PAIR OF CUT-OFF SWEATS and climbed onto his bed. The room he shared with Alex was little more than a glorified college dorm room, only bigger. At least the beds were full-size. And, like a dorm, they each had a set of drawers to put their clothes in, and a short rack for hanging items. Under the window between the two beds sat a desk, but only one. Elijah figured Niko didn't expect them to be getting a lot of work done between scenes.

It wasn't that late. And, if he was smart, he would get started on his Dynamic Systems homework before he got too far behind. He reached for his backpack and pulled out his laptop. He padded over to the desk, powered up his computer, and went to download his homework from the college's website.

As he waited for the site to load—which for a technological school, it had crappy technology—he clicked on a new tab and typed *Alex Payne*.

He scrolled down the list of results. The kid had a freaking *Wikipedia* page. Seriously? Looked like Sebastian knew something the rest of them didn't.

Slowly, Elijah scanned the *Wiki* page. It talked about Alex's high school baseball career. Talked about him being the number one draft pick his junior year of college after helping take his team to the College World Series in Omaha.

Elijah continued to scroll down. After Alex had been drafted by the Los Angeles Grizzlies, the team had started him immediately with the San Fernando Hawks Double-A baseball team. According to the scouts, Alex was a phenom and had been expected to rise through the ranks of Minor League Baseball in record time.

And Alex's signing bonus, in the neighborhood of six million dollars, reflected the Grizzlies' faith in their draft pick.

Almost six million dollars.

Elijah couldn't even wrap his mind around that kind of money. And with a signing bonus that high, what the hell was Alex doing at Black Stallion?

Elijah continued to read. The page had been populated with photos. Alex in high school. Alex's team lifting him up in victory after a win in Omaha. But it was the last photo that made Elijah's gut churn. It was a photo from Alex's Major League debut. But Alex wasn't smiling. A grimace etched his face, his jaw clenched as he clutched his right elbow. *Jesus Christ.*

Elijah caught movement out of the corner of his eye a fraction of a second before Alex slammed his hand down on Elijah's laptop lid. "What the fuck are you doing?"

Alex had his hands on his hips, a towel wrapped low around his waist, his face red. But the heat on Alex's face wasn't from taking a hot shower. His hair was damp, and beads of water dripped down his chest and disappeared beneath the towel. Elijah did his best not to follow the drops down.

With his hands held up in surrender, Elijah said, "Hey, man. I'm sorry. I didn't mean anything by it."

Alex scrubbed his hands through his hair scattering droplets of water onto the tiled floor. He blew out a deep breath. "No, man, it's okay. I—"

Dropping down on the corner of his bed, Alex continued, "That wasn't a very good time in my life. And if you have questions about it, I'd prefer you asked me instead of reading about it online. There's so much bullshit out there that isn't even close to being true."

Elijah swiveled in the desk chair, the springs creaking and complaining as he leaned back. "What are you doing here when you had a six million dollar signing bonus? I mean, I saw your car. The Challenger is nice, but it's not a Lambo. How could you blow through that much money in so little time?"

The color drained from Alex's face, and the spark died in front of Elijah's eyes. Asshole question? Yeah. What Alex had done with his money was none of Elijah's damn business.

"Scratch that. Forget I said anything. You don't owe me an explanation."

Alex stood and lifted his duffel bag onto his bed and started scrounging around for some clothes. "It's okay. I shouldn't get worked up about it. What happened to the money is no secret. If I'd have let you read any farther, you would have found out that my agent embezzled from me. I'm fighting him in court. At this point, I'm pretty sure the only people who are going to come out ahead are the lawyers."

Onto the bed, Alex dropped a pair of boxer briefs and athletic shorts. Then in the next moment, his towel fell to the floor and Elijah stared at the most magnificent, muscular, munchable ass he'd ever laid eyes on. He should look away. Really. Before he got caught ogling his straight roommate.

"You should warn a guy before you drop trou," Elijah said, mainly because he thought that's what a totally straight guy would say.

Over his shoulder, Alex glanced at Elijah with a stupid smile on his face as he stepped into his underwear. "You shy, Eli?"

Eli. A squeamish shiver ran down Elijah's spine. It kinda squicked him out to have a hot man use that name. "Only my mom calls me that."

Instead of an apology, that stupid grin pitched a tent and camped out on Alex's face. "Don't tell me you've never seen a man naked."

That pulled a laugh out of Elijah he hadn't known lurked near the surface. "I was in the military. Trust me, I've probably seen more dick and ass than all these gay porn stars combined."

"I grew up in locker rooms. I don't even think about it anymore. If it's a problem—"

"No," Elijah said, probably a little faster than he should have. A straight guy would have probably let the man finish his sentence. Heat rose up the back of his neck and he tried to ignore it. What did he really have to be embarrassed about? "I mean, do what you want. It's not like I'm not going to see you naked tomorrow. And then some."

Alex turned and Elijah watched as Alex adjusted the waistband of his shorts, admiring the V of hard muscle that arrowed beneath the elastic. It was then that Elijah felt Alex's eyes on him. Slowly, he looked up.

He'd expected embarrassment on Alex's face. Or perhaps anger. But when he looked into Alex's eyes, that's not what he saw. Alex's gaze heated and his focus flicked down to Elijah's lips and back again. "Yeah," Alex said at last. "And then some."

If Alex were a woman, Elijah would have taken him up on the blatant invitation. But this was his roommate. His *straight* roommate. Or maybe, like him, Alex had a touch of the bi.

Elijah broke eye contact first. He reopened the lid on his laptop and said, "I've got some homework I need to work on. Is this going to bug you? I could take it out to the lounge area."

"Not gonna bother me." Alex plugged in his phone charger, fluffed one of the pillows, and plopped down on top of the covers, his athletic shorts did little to hide what the man packed beneath it.

Jesus Christ, Maddox. Get your shit together, before everyone notices you're much too eager to shoot that extra scene with Alex than any straight guy should be.

The last thing Elijah needed was to be kicked off set before he got his first paycheck. Elijah closed the *Wikipedia* page, signed into his professor's class, and downloaded his homework. He pulled the textbook out of his backpack and turned to chapter five and got to work.

Elijah didn't know how long he'd been at it when Alex said, "You awake over there?"

Elijah glanced over his shoulder. Alex was propped up on the bed, one knee raised with an arm behind his head as he scrolled on his phone. Elijah made sure his gaze didn't drift down the long expanse of Alex's torso and all those long, lean muscles. "Yeah, why do you ask?"

"It's been twenty minutes, and you haven't even turned the first page. You dyslexic or something?"

Not dyslexic. *Distracted.* And the semi he'd been sporting behind his sweats ever since Alex dropped his towel hadn't helped either.

"No." Elijah closed his book. He wasn't getting anything done tonight, and he damn well knew it. "I guess I've got some things on my mind. Might as well go to bed. Seven is going to come early. Mind if I cut the lights?"

Alex laid his phone on the bedside table and scooted farther down the bed. "Go ahead. I could use the sleep as well."

Elijah turned out the lights, pitching the room into near darkness. The outside security lights shone through the slats of the blinds casting the room in a dull glow. "Want me to close the blinds?"

"Leave them."

Turning back the covers, Elijah crawled into bed. He settled back as the exhaustion kicked in. Not so much physical, but emotional exhaustion. The few weeks leading up to this trip to Black Stallion had been nerve-racking and had required a bit of soul searching. He hadn't been this on-edge about a new phase of his life since the night before he'd left for boot camp.

Eventually, Alex's breathing grew slow and even. Elijah stared out the window as a light mist dripped past the security light. His anxiety made the skin on his scalp tight, and if he were anywhere else, he'd do something proactive about the stiffy in his shorts.

If it wasn't for house rule number three: no jacking off before the shoot.

"Are you nervous?" Drowsiness thickened Alex's voice. Elijah had thought he was asleep.

Elijah rolled onto his side and looked over at his future scene mate. The dim light highlighted Alex's cheeks and his strong jawline, but the rest of his body remained in shadows.

"If I said I wasn't, I'd be lying. How about you?"

"On the nervousness scale, this hits somewhere between waiting to see where my name would fall in the draft and standing up on that mound in the big leagues for the first time. My heart feels like it's jacked up on speed, and my gut feels like I've eaten about two pounds of putrid pork."

"I'd definitely never imagined myself signing up to do porn."

Alex chuckled, low and rueful. "You can say that again, bro."

They fell into silence, but Elijah knew Alex hadn't fallen asleep. Not only because of the way Alex's foot bounced up and down, but by the nervous energy sparking off him like firecrackers on the Fourth of July.

Finally, Alex cleared his throat and said, "You ever kiss a guy?"

Where was Alex going with this? Elijah waited a beat before saying anything, not sure if he should answer with the partial truth, which was a no.

Or the whole truth.

That over the years he'd thought about it. A lot. But as much as he didn't want to hide who he really was, his marketability, his income, with Black Stallion required discretion. "No. Never."

"I don't know what I'm worried about more, kissing a guy, or kissing a guy and then freaking the fuck out on camera."

Alex didn't strike Elijah as homophobic, a guy would have to have some sort of open-mindedness to do gay porn to begin with. But the guy had initially signed up for a solo jack-off scene, not a scene with another guy, so, who knew.

"Look," Elijah said. "If you want to back out of our scene—"

"It's not that." Alex sat up, his legs coming over the edge of the bed to rest on the floor. "What do you think... Maybe we could..." Alex ran his hands through his hair and down his face. "*Fuuuck.*" His word came out quiet and subdued.

Alex stared across the room at Elijah, but in the shadows, his expression proved difficult to read. Again, Elijah had the feeling that Alex was one wrong word away from bolting, yet at the same time, it felt like Alex had reached out.

"I've got a solution." Elijah's dick said solution. His conscience said self-serving construct.

"What's that?" Alex sounded relieved, if not a tad skeptical.

"We could kiss. You know, kind of like a practice run. If after that, you want out, you can let Sebastian know in the morning."

Alex hesitated what under normal circumstances might have been a beat or two before answering, but with the way Elijah's pulse raced, the wait could have topped a hundred. "Okay."

If the house hadn't been so silent, if air had been blowing through the vents, Elijah wouldn't have heard him.

Alex didn't move. Neither did Elijah. Had Alex said 'Okay?' Or had Elijah's hearing of the word been dickful thinking?

They both stood at the same time. Alex smiled, slow and shy and sexy as hell. They met in the middle, halfway between this-is-a-good-idea and this-could-go-oh-so-bad.

What if Alex didn't like it?

What if *he* didn't like it?

Would that mean Elijah wasn't really into men? Or not into *this* man.

Yeah, and that semi you're sporting is because you find Dynamic Systems *homework so sexy.*

They stopped, inches apart. Alex's breathing coarse, halting, haphazard.

"This really what you want?" Elijah had to ask.

"Yes." Alex ducked his head, his hand reaching for Elijah's face, stopping short of contact.

At that moment, Elijah decided to go for what he wanted. He wrapped his fingers around Alex's neck, the tiny bristles from where it had been shaved from a recent haircut pricking his skin. Elijah's thumb trailed through the short stubble on Alex's jawline. The hair on Elijah's arms stood up, from excitement, not fear.

Alex inched closer and brushed his lips against Elijah's. Not a peck—a touch, a taste, before pulling back a fraction to gauge both of their reactions. Alex didn't run screaming from the room, so Elijah pulled him in for proper kiss.

Alex's lips were soft, yet firm and the scrape of Alex's scruff against Elijah's skin sent a zing down his spine and made his junk heavier.

More than anything, Elijah wanted to close the gap between

them, to grind against Alex's muscled thigh, to reach a hand down and cup the man before him.

Which kind of negated the supposition that maybe Elijah wasn't into men.

But he didn't dare.

He wanted Alex to come to him.

Elijah opened his mouth a fraction, inviting Alex in. Alex sucked in a breath through his nose, his tongue snaking out and touching Elijah's.

Elijah tamped down on the groan building at the back of his throat, refusing to let it free. Shifting, he angled his head to take the kiss deeper. Alex hissed in a breath. Whether it was from the way Elijah's tongue had invaded Alex's mouth or the way Elijah's erection brushed against Alex's thigh, Elijah couldn't be sure.

What Elijah did know for certain was that he wanted more.

Much more.

Of this.

Of Alex.

Elijah leaned into the kiss. One second Alex was there, the nape of his neck in Elijah's hand, his tongue in Elijah's mouth, his thigh pressed against Elijah's cock.

And then... nothing.

Alex had spun away, and Elijah took a step forward to catch his balance.

Alex leaned against the bedroom door, his hands covering his face in what Elijah could only read as a holy-shit-what-have-I-done kind of move.

"Hey, man... you okay?"

Elijah wanted to step closer, but that would have made him feel like the predator on the scent of injured prey.

Alex blew out a harsh lungful of air then straightened and took a step away from the door. "Yeah. I'm good. Um..." He made a motion with his hand between the two of them that Elijah assumed referred to them kissing. "Thanks."

"So... you good for tomorrow or do we need to talk to Sebastian?"

"No. I'm not going to pussy out."

"Scrote out." Elijah corrected.

"What?"

"Scrotums are weak. One wrong touch and they drop you to your knees. Pussies are tough. They swallow up sperm and spit out babies. So, if you're going to chicken out—"

Alex held up his hands and laughed. "I'm not *scroting* out."

"This from the guy who ran from a kiss."

"I didn't run."

Elijah raised his brows. In the low light, Alex probably couldn't see them well. Elijah's silence spoke well enough, all but calling him on it.

"I needed a second to wrap my head around it, is all." Alex brushed past Elijah and plopped down on his bed.

"You didn't like it?"

Alex's cheeks puffed out, and he blew out an exasperated breath. "I didn't *not* like it. And I have no idea what that means."

5

ALEX HAD BEEN TOO EXHAUSTED THE NIGHT BEFORE TO SPIRAL into some existential crisis about what it meant that not only had he *not* been repulsed by kissing Elijah, he quite liked it, if he admitted the truth only to himself. That existential crisis would have to wait until he got back home. There was so much other stuff going on at Black Stallion that gobbled up all of his emotional bandwidth.

From the time he'd woken up that morning, he and Elijah both pretended things weren't awkward, which only made things even more awkward. Breakfast had been quiet with the other men still in bed.

At the ass crack of dawn, they were showered and shaved per Niko's request, and he and Elijah had found their way to the studios in the basement of the performers' wing of the building.

Below ground, they were issued robes and instructed to change and head to hair and makeup, where both of their faces were powdered and their hair gelled and styled.

Besides the makeup room and the four stage areas for shooting scenes, there were two other rooms. A dressing room complete with showers for clean up after shoots, and the 'Ready room,' which was another name for a place full of straight porn, both in magazines and online. Something to get the blood pumping and the cocks hard.

Sebastian walked into makeup as Cat, a petite brunette complete with a brow piercing, tattoos, and a healthy dose of sass, made the finishing touches on Alex's hair.

"Okay, hotness," Cat said to Alex, "show those boys what you've got."

Sebastian glanced down at the clipboard in his hand, all business and no fangirling besides the flush that ran up the man's neck. "Alex, Niko has your scene first, then Elijah, then you two will have a break while Grant, Reyes, and Darius do a scene, then it will be back to you two. Sound good?"

"Sure." Alex tried hiding the note of panic in his voice. It wasn't that he wanted to back out of his solo scene, but if he'd had his choice, he would have liked to have Elijah go first, to see how it all went. But he wasn't a puss—scrote. He'd go first if that's what Niko wanted.

"Fine by me," Elijah said as Cat washed her hands and went to get started on his hair.

"Alex, you're with me," Sebastian said, "Niko's ready."

Sebastian led Alex down the hall to one of the stages that was all lit up with bright lights. The set consisted of three walls, the fourth one open for lighting and filming. Inside, sat a beige leather couch, a side table with a lamp, and a nondescript carpet in front.

Which pretty much looked like the set of most jack-off porn he'd seen.

Niko didn't waste time on pleasantries. When Alex arrived on set, Niko introduced the cameraman. "Vin, this is Alex. Alex, Vin."

Alex would have shaken the man's hand, but Vin's were full with a camera and other gear. "Nice to meet you, man."

"You, too." Vin turned to Niko and said, "This is the guy we're shooting from the neck down, yeah?"

"Yeah," Niko said, half distracted as he consulted with Rose about something.

Vin bobbed his head toward the set and Alex followed. "Should I know you from somewhere?"

It was almost a relief not to be recognized. "Not really. Not anymore. Niko's being extra cautious, which I appreciate."

"Leave the robe there." Vin pointed at a hook on the wall at the entrance to the set.

When Alex did, Sebastian came over and said, "Pull up the waistband on the jockstrap and let the athletic shorts drop low on your hips."

Along with the pair of navy-blue athletic shorts, he'd been given a jockstrap. As a baseball player, he wasn't a stranger to them, but usually they were plain white or black and had an opening in the fabric to hold a cup for protection.

This *thing* he'd put on was *not* for protection.

There was so little of the light-blue material, that it had taken him a few minutes to make sure all his bits were covered.

Which, frankly now that he thought about it, seemed like a waste of time and effort considering he was about to get naked in front of the camera.

Alex did as Sebastian requested and hitched up the jock-strap's waistband, the words *King Dong* emblazoned across the white elastic. Sebastian glanced over, and Alex turned to see Elijah come down the hall.

Sebastian walked toward Elijah. "There are a few seats behind the lights if you want to watch." Then to Alex, "You good with him watching?"

Alex thought about saying no. There were already going to be at least four or five other people, strangers practically, on set from what Alex could see, all watching him jack himself. Did he really need the pressure of another set of eyes on him?

But then he glanced over at Elijah. His roommate. His future scene-mate. The man he'd kissed the night before and didn't hate it.

Didn't hate it? Pretty sure the semi you've had in your pants since the moment he put his lips on you means you did more than not hate it.

And really, of all of them, Elijah was the closest person on the set he could consider a friend. "It's fine. He can stay."

Elijah gave him the briefest of nods and Alex turned away to hide the hint of a smile that curved his lips.

Niko extracted himself from Rose and met with Alex on the set. "So, this is how it's going to go. We'll start with you on the couch, I'll ask you a few questions so the viewers can get to know you a bit, some of them dig that shit. Then you can start stroking yourself. First with your shorts on, then we'll have you take the shorts off, do some shooting with the jockstrap. Then we'll lose that, too. Any questions?"

Alex knew he should probably have some, but with his brain hyper-focused on keeping the jitters at bay, he couldn't think of anything to ask. "I don't think so."

"I like to give as little direction as possible on the solo scenes. You do your thing, and if something needs changing, I'll let you know. Capiche?"

"Got it."

Niko took one step away and then turned back around. "You need a few minutes in the Ready room, first?"

Between his recent streak of celibacy, the kiss with Elijah the night before, and remembering the feel of Elijah's hard dick against his thigh, Alex didn't think he'd have any trouble getting it up. He only hoped he wouldn't come too soon and embarrass himself. Did he get paid less if he busted his nut in the first thirty seconds?

"I think I'm good."

Niko extended his hand toward the couch for Alex to have a seat, then turned away. "Okay, places everybody."

Alex took a seat on the couch and tried to swallow. For a guy whose previous profession included a lot of spitting, his mouth was unnaturally dry.

Vin moved in closer with his camera. "At some point, I'll be all up in your business. Don't focus on me. Focus on the job."

Alex nodded, afraid a croak would escape instead of words if he tried to speak.

Niko's voice boomed across the set. "Action."

———

"Cut!" Niko hollered out.

Vin dropped the camera from his shoulder as Niko walked onto the set. Alex's head fell back, not in ecstasy, but in obvious exasperation.

Elijah had found a place in the shadows out of the way to watch Alex's scene. Even though Alex had given him permission to be there, that moment's hesitation before Alex had given his consent couldn't be ignored and he hadn't wanted to add any more pressure.

"What now?" Alex let his hand drop from his cock. His very nice, very large cock, if Elijah were the judge.

Niko stepped closer to Alex, but with the mic boom above them, his words traveled. "You've got to relax. Get out of your head."

"I am relaxed."

"No, you're not. Your legs are practically clamped together, your jaw is clenched, and you're only half-hard."

Alex blew out a breath. "Sorry, man. This is a lot harder than I'd thought."

"The first time is always the hardest." Niko's voice had dropped, but not enough that the mics didn't pick it up. "Forget I'm here, forget Vin's here. Forget everyone's here and focus on your dick."

Niko glanced at his watch. "You think you can do that? Or do you need to go back to the Ready room?"

"No." Alex's expression shifted from frustration to determination. "I can do this."

Niko slowly backed away. "Okay. Take a moment. Stand up. Shake the tension out of your arms and legs, then get your head back into whatever space you need to go to get it done."

Niko walked back out of camera range, and Alex stood and loosened himself up. At this point in the shoot, he was completely naked. Alex worked his neck from side to side and shook the tension out of his arms, but it was Alex's semi-erect cock that got Elijah's full attention.

Elijah shifted and reached down to adjust himself in the jockstrap he'd been given, already close to busting a nut. At this rate, his own scene would be shot in record time.

He probably should walk off the set to give his erotic imagination a chance to cool off, but one glance at Alex as he stroked a hand down himself and yeah... Elijah wasn't going anywhere.

Cat from makeup walked by, her eyes on Alex, and Alex's on her. "Wow, nice cock, dude."

Alex grinned, giving himself another couple of pumps and his cock was rock hard again.

"Hey, Cat?" Niko asked in a pretty-please voice. "Can you do me a favor?"

"Nuh, uh," Cat said, "I'm not going to be Alex's visual fluffer."

"Awh, come on. I rarely ask—"

"You give me that paid week off I asked for at the end of the month, and I'll do it."

"Two days."

"Four, my clothes stay on, and you've got yourself a deal." Cat smiled, like... well, the porn cat that ate the canary. She knew she had Niko by the wallet.

"Four days," Niko agreed.

She turned toward Alex. "Tits or ass, hot stuff?"

Alex laughed as he sat on the couch again. "Ass."

Cat turned around and gave Elijah a wink. Her blouse was cut dangerously low in the front, and her skirt was so short Elijah was pretty sure if she bent over, Alex would see all the goods as well.

"You're okay with this?" Elijah asked, though she didn't really seem put out.

"Are you kidding me? Four paid days off for something that guys walking down the street do all the time for free? Hells yeah."

Cat cocked her hip and glanced over her shoulder at Alex whose eyes had locked on that cute little ass of hers. Elijah had a hard time not picturing her as the soft filling between him and Alex.

From the cup of her bra, Cat pulled out her phone and scrolled through an app while Alex beat himself off. Even without the microphones, Elijah would have been able to hear the unmistakable sound of flesh on flesh, and the rough and raw groans escaping the back of Alex's throat.

Elijah couldn't take his eyes off Alex, his own hand reaching down to his junk. Then Alex's gaze shifted and focused on him. Alex's eyes went wide for a fraction as if he'd only now noticed Elijah standing there.

Elijah didn't look away. He couldn't. A cocky smile slowly

spread across Alex's face, his hand working harder, faster. His breathing, as well as Elijah's own, going ragged.

In those moments before Alex's head fell back and he came, it wasn't Cat's ass that Alex was staring at, but Elijah.

———

"And cut! That's a wrap," Niko said.

Alex stopped stroking himself. With his head resting on the back of the couch, he stared up at the high ceiling trying to catch his breath as his cock went soft in his hand.

A warm, damp towel landed on his chest. He glanced up to see Sebastian standing there. "Go ahead and get yourself cleaned up, catch a shower, and relax. You've got at least a couple of hours before your next scene."

"Sure. Thanks." Alex didn't look Sebastian in the eye. Instead he glanced past Sebastian's shoulder to where Elijah had been.

But Elijah was gone.

Surreptitiously, Alex glanced around, but no Elijah.

There had been a moment there when his and Elijah's eyes had connected, and Alex had felt that same pull, that same erotic tension that he'd felt the night before when he'd kissed Elijah.

And Elijah had kissed him back.

Cat's ass, which was an objectively fine ass, one that most of his ex-teammates would have killed to get their hands on, hadn't been doing it for Alex.

What had been doing it was Elijah's unapologetic, heated gaze. That unveiled lust that had shoved Alex over the edge of climactic inevitability like a full-on body slam, his muscles, his mind, reeling.

His limbs wobbled, and his hands shook as he cleaned his

spunk off his belly.

"Nice job. Good to get the first one under your belt." Niko handed Alex his robe. "What did you think of your first experience?"

"Honestly, it takes a bit of getting used to. It was easier to forget the rest of you were there, but the camera all up in my business was a little unnerving."

"The more you come back, the easier and more natural it will feel."

If he comes back.

If? You need the money, Payne. If you want any chance of standing on that mound again, of hearing the crowd cheer your name, of watching the eyes of the guy at the plate widen when your heater freezes them in the batter's box. If you want any of that ever again, you have to keep up your sessions with Trevor. Which takes money.

Unless you really want to kiss baseball goodbye.

Which he didn't.

Which meant—like Schwarzenegger was so good at saying —he'd be back.

Niko pointed to a lined laundry hamper. "Used towels go over there. Check back in an hour or so. We should have a better idea when your scene with Elijah will start. You can go back to the residence and chill, or you're welcome to hang out here, watch some of the other scenes, see how the pros get it done. Either way, you'll need to see Cat again before the next shoot."

"Okay." Alex slipped into his robe. He went to shake Niko's hand, then realized that probably wouldn't be welcomed considering where his right hand had been five minutes ago.

Alex gathered the shorts and jockstrap and put them in a separate laundry bin from his wash rag, then headed down the hall to catch a shower. He checked the dressing room first. The other guys were there, but no Elijah. Next, he stuck his head into the makeup room, not sure why he was seeking his roommate out. To tell him to break a leg maybe?

Or ask him why he ran off?

Cat was alone in the room, folding towels. "Hey, Cat. You seen Elijah?"

"Should be around here somewhere. I just finished his touch-ups." She bobbed her chin in the general direction of his crotch. "Nice work out there."

Alex rolled his eyes. "Yeah. Sorry about that."

Cat hadn't been the one to do it for him. She didn't know that, but he wanted to acknowledge her willingness to help. "Thanks for the assist."

Maybe that thanks should go to Elijah. Maybe you should go find him and tell him...

What? What are you going to tell him?

Hell, he didn't have a clue.

That spark when he and Elijah had kissed, and getting off watching Elijah watch *him* didn't mean he was now into dudes.

Maybe he had an exhibitionist kink he hadn't known about.

Besides, Alex had sex with women.

Which meant he was straight. Right?

And while he couldn't say the sex had been earth-shattering, soul-transforming sex, it had been... *pleasurable* at least. Which only meant that he hadn't met the right woman yet.

And thinking that someone found you attractive, was *hot*, no matter which sex that person belonged to.

Cat snapped her fingers in front of his face. "You in there?"

Alex pulled his head out of the deep, dark cavern of denial that was his ass. "Sorry. You say something?"

She leaned a hip against her makeup counter and went back to folding towels. "I said if you ever want to thank me properly, give me a buzz."

What? "Um... yeah. Sure. I'll do that. Totally." And he'd shut up now before he made a complete, dorkified fool of himself. *Smooth, Payne. Real smooth. Good to see you haven't lost your touch with the ladies.*

What touch exactly, he didn't know. He wasn't like some of the other guys on his team who'd slept their way through every city the team traveled to. It wasn't that Alex hadn't been interested per se, it was that he'd been too focused on his career, and then on his recovery, to have much time for catting around.

You still telling yourself that tired lie?

As he climbed the stairs to the residence, ladies weren't on his mind. Not even a little bit. Men were. Or better said, *a* man.

Elijah wasn't in their shared room, or the lounge, or the kitchen, or the showers. Had he scared Elijah the fuck off? Would Alex have a second scene after all?

He and Elijah needed to talk. About what, Alex wasn't so sure. Maybe Elijah's attraction had been a figment of Alex's imagination all along. With Elijah standing in the shadows, Alex could have imagined the heat and lust in Elijah's eyes.

Unable to locate Elijah, Alex headed to the communal bathroom with the bank of stalls and showers in the residence area. Alex didn't rush his shower or dawdle. By the time he'd gotten cleaned and dressed—for the time being—he made it back down to the studio to a cacophony of whistles and catcalls as Elijah shrugged into his robe.

Alex had missed Elijah's scene. That had to have been some kind of record. What did they do? Shoot it all in one take?

Reyes, Darius, and Grant were all standing around dressed in work pants and shirts, their arms and faces dirt and grease stained and made to look like they'd recently finished their shift at the local mechanic shop.

"Watch out, Grant," Reyes said, "Elijah's gonna be getting that room to himself if he keeps that up."

"It was a jack-off scene," Grant muttered. "My grandmother couldn't mess that up."

"Yeah, man," Darius whooped and clapped his hands over his head. "A fucking natural. Hey, Niko, sign me up for a scene with this dog. That shit's gonna get some massive views."

Niko had his head together with Rose over some paperwork she had in her hand and didn't hear Darius. Not that Darius seemed to care.

Reyes started in on Grant. "I've seen your grandmother, she—"

"Don't." Grant cut him a look that could have stripped the hide off an elephant and tanned it in an instant.

With a sheepish smile, Elijah joined everyone off set while Sebastian and Vin prepared a different set for the next shoot. A shoot which apparently would involve a three-way with Darius, Grant, and Reyes.

That might be interesting.

Elijah glanced at Alex across the group of men, his smile shifting. The intensity of Elijah's gaze made Alex look away. Not from intimidation, but from arousal. What the actual fuck?

You're on the set of a porn studio, the air is already supercharged and erotic. Any man, gay or straight, couldn't help but be turned on in this environment.

Yeah. Alex would keep telling himself that until he believed it.

"Okay, everybody." Niko's voice boomed, echoing off the walls and the high ceiling. "Time to get back to work. Darius and Reyes, we're starting with the two of you."

Grant hung back as Darius gave Reyes a playful shove as they headed for the new set. "Hey, man, you heat up that beef tamale? If you're gonna fuck me, I don't want some limp—"

"Fuck you, man." Reyes shouldered him back with a laugh.

"That's what I'm saying."

Reyes turned and walked backward. "Hey, Vinny, make sure you've got that fish-eye lens, so my fans don't need a magnifier to see Darius' junk."

"*Jesus Christ*," Grant grumbled, "I know five-year-olds who are more mature than you dickheads."

As Elijah headed to a refreshment table set up in the back, Sebastian pulled Grant aside a few steps, but not so far Alex couldn't overhear.

"Hey, babe." Sebastian laid a hand on Grant's shoulder, but Grant shrugged him off.

"I told you not to call me that." Grant's eyes snagged on Alex then kept on moving, settling somewhere in the shadows on the far side of the studio.

"I... Are you all right? You seem a little... on edge. Even for you." Sebastian added a soft chuckle as if that would help ease the blow of the dig.

"Got a call from my grandmother." A statement, not an invitation for an interrogation.

Sebastian must have missed the not-so-subtle tone. "Everything okay?"

Grant rubbed a hand across his stubbled jaw, smearing the fake grime Cat had applied. "It's—"

Grant caught Alex staring, and Alex stepped away, giving them their privacy, but he managed to catch Grant's words when he said, "It's nothing. Some personal shit."

"If there's..."

Alex wandered out of earshot. This wasn't any of his business. Elijah walked up to him and offered a bottle of water. "Thanks, man."

On set, Vin adjusted the lighting while Niko watched one of the monitors. Sebastian and Grant were talking, their voices growing louder and carrying.

No one paid Alex or Elijah any attention. As Alex tipped the bottle of water back, he caught Elijah staring at the play of his throat while he drank. That question burned in Alex's mind again. The one that wanted to know why Elijah had disappeared after Alex's scene.

Alex wiped his mouth with the back of his hand. Essentially, they were alone, but he dropped his voice. "Where did you—"

Grant gave Sebastian a push that set the slighter man back a step. "What I *need*, Bass, is some fucking space." His booming voice reverberated in the open space.

Everyone on set turned and stared.

"If you need some time off, I'm sure—"

"What I *need* is to work." Grant's gaze landed like mini grenades on every person on set, one after the other, like little bombs of caustic emotion and cutting shrapnel. "Anyone here got a problem with that?"

"*Grant.*" Niko had that tone that couldn't be ignored. That tone that could mow grown men down to size. "Take five. Get your mind right, and come back here ready to work, capiche?"

"Yes, sir." Grant's gaze raked across Sebastian one final time as he turned and stormed off down the hall, the meat of his fist hitting the wall as he passed with an echoing, emphatic, frustrated, "*Fuck.*"

Niko turned back to the set. "Alright boys, let's get this done."

"Dude's got issues," Alex mumbled to Elijah.

"You telling me you've never had an off day?" Sebastian said as he walked by. The fangirl had vanished, and the protective momma bear growled. Alex could practically feel the scrape of unsheathed claws across his back.

"Quiet on the set," Niko hollered out and turned his attention to Reyes and Darius who had been uncharacteristically quiet during and after Grant's blowup. "And action."

Alex and Elijah settled in to watch. The set looked like an

auto repair shop, complete with a fuckable height tool chest, chain hoists, and a souped-up, cherry red, '57 Chevy Nova.

Against the backdrop, Reyes and Darius kissed and stripped and sucked. Niko cut in for direction once or twice, and at different times, Reyes and Darius had to go to the Ready room when their boners flagged.

By the time Grant came through the set's fake door some-time later, Darius had Reyes bent over the tool chest, pounding him from behind.

Elijah stood so near, the heat radiated from his body like a banked fire looking for a breath of air to spark it off. The heat reminded Alex of his scene and Elijah's subsequent disap-pearing act. "Where did you go after... after I'd finished. When I looked up..."

Elijah shifted, and his hard-on brushed against Alex's thigh. Alex's blood heated, the rest of the sentence evaporated from his brain.

"You wanna know why my shoot went so fast?"

That wasn't what Alex had asked, but yeah, he'd bite. "You're a natural?"

"Hardly. I was as nervous up there as you were."

Elijah's voice dipped and turned into a gruff whisper that made Alex's balls heavy as if they hadn't been drained in weeks.

That close, Alex caught the faint scent of musk and sweat clinging to Elijah's skin. "It was your shoot."

Gah. The sexual alchemy made Alex's wood turn to steel. He cleared his throat. "Yeah?" Alex kept his eyes on the scene unfolding on the set, but his focus remained on Elijah.

Elijah leaned in, his breath warm on Alex's neck. "Yeah. It made me hard as fuck."

6

———

Grant took a bite of a roast beef sandwich and tucked it into the pouch of his cheek. "I owe you all an apology."

Everyone had gathered up at the residence for the lunch Sebastian had catered in. Niko and Rose sat at opposite ends. Elijah sandwiched himself between Alex and Sebastian on one side of the table, while Reyes, Darius, and Grant sat on the other. A chair short, Vin had pulled up an extra chair and squeezed in at one of the corners.

Grant chewed up the bite and swallowed, his gaze going to Sebastian who'd sat as far away from Grant as he could get. "You especially, Bass. That wasn't one of my finer moments."

"It's cool." By Sebastian's flat tone, and the way he looked past Grant instead of at him, Grant's actions were far from 'cool.' Ever since Grant's blowup, the normal, upbeat Sebastian had remained decidedly subdued.

From the end of the table, Niko said, "As much as this is a job, we're also family here. You need something, you ask, capiche?"

"That go for all of us, or just stud muffin down there?" Darius asked, his eyes lit with their usual mischief.

"Speaking of *muffins*," Reyes piped in, "After that scene with Grant, mine is—"

Rose dropped her salad fork. "We're eating, Reynaldo. No one wants to hear about your raw ass."

"Jesus, I didn't mean anything by it." Reyes' voice deflated as if Rose had stuck a pin in him and burst his bubble.

Darius helped himself to some of the sliced apples. "Yeah, besides, man, you keep talking like that and you'll scare the new kids away."

Beside Elijah, Alex chuckled and shifted in his seat, his muscled thigh coming into contact with Elijah's. Elijah's nerves pinged, and the zap must have short-circuited his salivary glands because his mouth went dry and he had to gulp water to get his bite of the sandwich down.

Was Alex man-spreading or was the contact intentional?

"You okay over there?" Alex asked Elijah with the innocence of a kid, though that spark in his denim blue eyes relayed the exact opposite. Alex didn't shy from the contact, he twined his lower leg behind Elijah's.

Elijah's brain flashed to that moment during Alex's scene when Alex had stood and shaken the tension from his long limbs. Even when Alex's dick had been at half-mast, everything about that man turned Elijah's crank.

From Alex's long and lean athletic body to the muscle mass and visible veins, to the tiny bee tattoo on his left ribcage, to the deepest blue eyes Elijah had ever seen, and to that openness, that curiosity buried deep within them.

Whatever that attraction was, for once Elijah had no intention of fighting it. Who says you can't enjoy your work?

Glancing at the clock above the stove, Elijah counted down the minutes until he and Alex would shoot their scene together. He couldn't wait to get his hands, his lips, his tongue, his mouth, on the man pressed calf to thigh up against him.

Elijah wanted to hear Alex growl and groan as he gave him pleasure. Wanted to feel the heat of Alex's body, feel the pulse of his release, and taste the salt in his sweat and cum.

Alex bumped Elijah with his knee. Right. Alex had asked him if he was okay.

"I'm—" Elijah's voice squeaked worse than when he'd first hit puberty. The bastard was enjoying seeing Elijah squirm. He cleared his throat. "Fine."

Elijah turned his attention back to the ongoing conversation. Reyes pushed his plate away. "I'm just saying, stud muffin over there *really* gets into his role." Reyes bobbed his chin, indicating Grant. "If I didn't know he was straight, I'd think he was actually enjoying himself."

Grant beaned Reyes with a cherry tomato from his salad, his lips curving up a fraction. "It's called acting, numbnuts. That's what Niko pays me for. I can sell it. My ratings would be crap if it didn't come across as *real*."

———

An hour later found Vin and Sebastian prepping the same set Elijah and Alex had used for their solo scenes for their dual scene. When Vin had the lighting ready, he turned to Niko and said, "Ready when you are, boss."

Niko's expression flattened. "You know that makes me feel old when you call me that."

Vin reminded Elijah of the lanky emo kid from high school with the all black clothes, and the too-long hair, and skin too thick, and the quiet emotions that ran too deep. The kind of kid that held a façade up to the world so no one could see the real person behind it.

Come to think of it, Vin *probably had been* that kid.

All grown up, but still closed off.

But there was light in Vin's eyes and perhaps a hint of a grin on his lips when he said, "Yeah, I know."

"I should have left you on the streets where I found you." Affection, not malice, laced Niko's words.

Vin lifted his camera, an uncharacteristic full smile on his face as he turned toward the set. "Probably, boss, probably."

"Alex, Elijah, we're going to start with you two on the couch." Then to Vin, Niko said, "Remember, neck down on Alex. You can shoot them kissing from behind Alex's head."

"Got it," Vin replied.

Cat had dressed Elijah in a black designer T-shirt and cargo shorts, while Alex had been given athletic shorts and a Clippers T-shirt that showed off his athletic body. Elijah followed Alex onto the set, and his eyes kept drifting to the drape of fabric over Alex's fine ass.

The ass that Elijah hadn't been able to get out of his head ever since Alex had dropped his towel the night before. His fingers itched to grab it, his teeth wanted to bite it.

They'd both just come from the Ready room, but damn, the porn hadn't gotten him nearly as aroused as the view before Elijah now.

They both sat on the couch. Half a cushion separated them. Elijah didn't know if he should get closer or—

"Scoot together," Niko said.

They scooted.

"More."

When they touched from hip to knee, Niko said, "That's good."

Similar to their solo scenes, Niko asked them both some questions from off camera aimed to help them relax and viewers to get to know them a little. Beside him, Alex sat stiff, his answers stilted as he wiped his palms on his thighs and tugged at the hem of his shorts.

After a series of questions to each of them, Niko asked Elijah, "Why did you want to do a scene with Alex?"

They hadn't been given the questions ahead of time. Niko wanted the answers to sound natural, not memorized. Elijah didn't have to think hard to come up with a response. "I've seen his work. I'm a big fan."

Alex had been looking straight ahead. A flush rushed up the back of his neck, and he turned to look at Elijah. Damn... those deep, denim eyes...

Elijah wanted the lights and the camera and the mics to disappear, but that wasn't about to happen, so he pushed them from his mind and did his best to focus on the man beside him. Cat had done a damn fine job with Alex's hair. He had that surfer boy, just-fucked-and-out-of-bed look to him, though they'd been up since the butt crack of dawn.

Elijah couldn't get past the idea that he wanted to be the one to make Alex look like that for real.

"Kiss him," Niko directed.

But Elijah had already eased forward, running his thumb across the faint stubble growing along Alex's jawline. Alex leaned into the touch, his eyes drifting closed as Elijah pulled him in for a kiss. Those lips. Tender. Tempting. Tantalizing.

This time, Elijah didn't hold back the groan as Alex opened his mouth and deepened the kiss. Alex's hands fisted in Elijah's shirt, tugging him closer, forcing Elijah to balance himself with a hand on Alex's muscled thigh.

He wanted to ease his hand higher, to cup Alex's balls, and to feel the thickness of Alex's shaft in his hands. His own dick strained against his jock, and his pre-cum moistened the material.

Niko interrupted only long enough to say, "Shirts."

Elijah broke the kiss, his breath coming faster as he reached back and yanked the shirt over his head and tossed it aside. His grin widened at Alex's heated, hooded gaze as Alex reached out and ran a finger down Elijah's sternum. His eyes fell closed at the touch, imagining other places he'd like those fingers.

His own hands went to Alex's chest. Even though Alex's muscles flexed beneath his hand, when he opened his eyes again, he almost expected Alex not to be there, that he'd spun away like he'd done in their room the night before.

This time, the look in Alex's eyes had shifted, a little less stunned, a little more predatory.

Oh, hell yeah. This was going to be fun.

Elijah grabbed the hem of Alex's shirt and eased it up Alex's long torso, letting his fingers trail up Alex's sides. They bumped along his rib cage, and goosebumps erupted all over Alex's flesh. It gave Elijah a thrill seeing what his touch did to him.

And if the goosebumps weren't enough evidence of Alex's arousal, the bulge in Alex's shorts provided definitive proof. Alex pulled Elijah back into the kiss, this time taking, demanding, devouring more.

The tug of Alex's grip in Elijah's hair sent a shiver of delicious pain across his scalp that had Elijah doubling down on the kiss, loving the contrast between pain and pleasure.

As much as he enjoyed the kissing and Alex's fingers in his hair, Elijah craved more contact. He eased his fingers up Alex's thigh, beneath the loose fabric of his shorts and cupped Alex through his jock. Alex broke the kiss with a hiss, his head falling back, his grip tightening in Elijah's hair.

"Fuck yeah," Alex groaned, his pre-cum starting to drench his jock.

Elijah hated for all that pre-cum to go to waste, not when it could be slicking his hands and Alex's shaft.

Shifting, Elijah dropped to his knees between Alex's legs, his hands going to the waistband of Alex's shorts. Alex's breath caught, his gaze intense as he glanced down at Elijah. Elijah raised a brow, a silent ask for permission, though permission had been granted when they'd signed on the dotted line the day before.

But contract or no contract, Elijah wanted to be confident he and Alex were on the same page. Saying you were willing to let a guy suck your cock in theory might become too much of a reality when a guy settled between your legs.

Their eyes locked for a beat, the slight nod Alex gave made more potent by its pointed precision. Vin moved in with the camera. Elijah had almost forgotten he was there. For the most part, it seemed that Niko's style was to allow the scene to unfold naturally between the broad strokes of what had been agreed upon earlier rather than give constant direction.

Which, as a newbie, Elijah appreciated.

Alex raised his hips, and Elijah pulled his shorts and jock down together, Alex's cock catching on the elastic waistband before popping free.

Sweet baby Jesus.

If Elijah was going to suck a cock for the first time, this was the one to suck. Greeks would have made marble statues of it. Carving it in stone to save perfection for posterity. Elijah glanced up, checking in one last time.

"Go on," Alex said, his voice like honey over gravel—sweet and at the same time, infinitely gritty and hard.

Skimming his hands up Alex's thighs, Elijah kept his eyes trained on Alex's face, wanting to watch his expression as a man took hold of him for the first time. Elijah wanted to see what he could do to Alex, what he could make him feel, but most of all, he wanted to make sure that he stopped if Alex changed his mind.

Elijah spanned a hand over Alex's lower abdomen, enjoying the quake of the muscles beneath his hand, enjoying the moment as the erotic tension thickened. Alex's jaw clenched, sweat formed on his chest, and pre-cum beaded at his slit.

"You scroting out on me?" Alex grumbled, probably too quiet for the mics to pick up.

Elijah moved his hand toward Alex's jutting cock. "Oh, hell no."

———

OH, HELL NO.

Alex liked the sound of that. For a moment there, he'd thought Elijah was going to be the one to wuss out. He'd thought Elijah's hesitation meant he'd had reservations, but then that grin Elijah got had made Alex's pulse knock and his cock throb.

Sweat ran down Alex's sternum. Not so much from the lights, but from the anticipation of getting Elijah's hands on him. His nerves thrummed—this high-capacity buzz energizing his system like an electric surge on a high-power line.

Elijah's thumb swiped through the pre-cum on his tip, slicking the moisture across the head, the touch light and teasing. Alex's eyes fluttered closed for a count of three as he blew out a breath. When he opened his eyes again, Elijah was there checking in with him, a pinch of worry in his eyes.

But Alex wasn't panicking. It felt too damn good. A hand was a hand was a hand. Right?

Only Elijah's hand was like no other he'd had on his dick before. The fingers were broad and blunt, the grip firmer, more... experienced? Alex shouldn't have been surprised, as Elijah eased his hand down Alex's shaft again and again. After all, who better to know how a guy liked to be stroked and gripped and teased than another guy? Than someone who'd spent the last ten to fifteen years masturbating and learning exactly what it took to make a guy come?

Elijah's strokes became firmer, faster, as Alex leaked pre-cum like the Trevi Fountain. Rising on his knees, Elijah sucked Alex's nipple into his mouth. The sensation sent a zing to Alex's groin, and he bucked up into Elijah's hands.

Alex gripped the back of Elijah's head, holding Elijah in place. Alex's breath came in short bursts as his climax built.

And built.

Alex's hips pistoned faster. If they were going to get the blow job in before he came, Elijah better damn well hurry. With a hand on Elijah's shoulder, Alex guided him down, too hot, too aroused, too orgasmic to think about the fact a guy was about to suck his cock. He'd have time to process what that all meant later. Right now, all he wanted was release.

Now.

Elijah worked his way down Alex's torso. Slowly. Too slowly.

"Hurry," Alex managed, more a strangled mash-up of consonants and vowels than an actual word.

Instead of immediately going down on him, Elijah stopped his strokes, his fingers gently brushing down Alex's shaft. Alex groaned in frustration. "Bastard."

Elijah chuckled. Reaching up, he pulled Alex in for a scorching kiss that was all attitude, tongue, and testosterone. Elijah broke the kiss, his eyes steady on Alex's as he gripped Alex's base and eased back down on his haunches.

Alex's hips pumped as he ached for that first touch of Elijah's mouth—the feel of those lips easing over his sensitive head. Elijah's tongue darted out first for a taste, a bold and brash smile coming to that fuckable mouth. Then Elijah rounded the ridge of Alex's cock with the tip of his tongue.

Alex sucked in a breath. And held it. And held it.

What the fuck was he doing?

He was straight. Perfectly... straight.

Then why does the sight of your dick sliding into a man's mouth make you hard enough to cut steel?

Alex grabbed Elijah on either side of his head, his fingers wrapping around the soft, short strands of hair, not knowing whether he'd planned to push him away...

Or hold him there.

That tortuous mouth... that playful tongue.

Damn.

Alex's head fell back, his breath coming in crisp, harsh pants as Elijah's talented tongue brought him closer and closer to the brink. He tried to imagine there was a woman going down on him, but no woman had ever given him head the way Elijah was.

Or maybe it had nothing to do with Elijah. Maybe his enhanced arousal had to do with other people watching.

That a camera focused on his crotch.

That the mics picked up the soft, wet sounds of sucking and the low groan escaping the back of his throat making the experience so... fucking... hot.

Elijah worked hard with his hands and his mouth bringing Alex to that knife edge, Alex's hips thrusting as his dick hit the back of Elijah's throat.

"*Fuuuck.*" As much as Alex wanted to hold out, he wasn't the one in control. His balls tightened, and the base of his spine tingled as the first pulses hit.

"I'm coming," Alex ground out as he tried to pull Elijah off him. Instead of finishing Alex off with his hand the way Alex had expected, Elijah took him impossibly deep, relaxing the back of his throat, his lips going down to Alex's root.

"*Fuck, fuck.*" Alex's vocabulary had shrunk to one word. "*Fuuuck.*"

If you could only have one word, that one said enough.

Elijah swallowed it all. Pulling back, the flat of Elijah's

tongue raked along the underside of Alex's cock until it fell free. With a cum-eating grin and open mouth kisses, Elijah worked his way up Alex's body. Elijah nipped Alex on the tender flesh between his neck and shoulder then sucked away the sting, taking Alex's hand in his and pulling him to his feet.

Alex had to lock his knees to keep from collapsing, his body slack, sucked, and sated.

But they weren't done. Elijah hadn't come.

With his hands cupping Alex's face, Elijah pulled him in for an open mouth kiss, their tongues dueling. Alex tasted the saltiness of himself on Elijah's tongue, smelled the tang of sweat and musk of sex.

God, that man could kiss.

It was like Elijah poured all of his emotion into the kiss until Alex could practically taste Elijah's excitement, his attraction, his arousal. Elijah didn't kiss just to kiss. He was a hundred percent present in the moment, taking Alex in.

Even though Alex had barely recovered from coming for the second time that day, he hadn't gone entirely soft.

Now it was his turn to pleasure Elijah.

His hands shook as he reached for the button on Elijah's shorts. Elijah dropped his hand to Alex's, his other wrapped around Alex's head and pulled him in close, their chests touching, their sweat sliding and mixing together as the stage lights beat down on them like a Sahara summer sun.

Out of the corner of his eye, Alex caught Vin kneeling with his camera, shooting upward from the ground.

Elijah whispered in Alex's ear. "You don't have to do this."

Alex swallowed hard. He'd never touched another man's cock. But it was a job, right? Niko was paying them both a wad of cash because that's what it took to get a straight guy to jack and suck another guy off.

This didn't mean anything.

Being curious about what it would feel like to have another man in his hands, to bring him pleasure the way Elijah had brought pleasure and satisfaction to him, didn't have to mean anything either.

He could do this and still call himself straight, like Grant, Reyes, and Darius all did.

In answer, Alex pulled back and brushed Elijah's staying hand away, worked the button free, and took the zipper down inch by inch. Elijah rested his forehead on Alex's shoulder and swallowed with an audible click, his breath already coming faster.

Elijah reached down and dropped his shorts and jock over his hips and kicked them away.

God, he was really doing this.

"You don't—" Elijah started to say again until Alex's hand closed around Elijah's shaft, his words dying with a groan.

The girth felt foreign in Alex's hand. He hadn't expected that. As well as the slight curvature at the tip. He ran his thumb up the prominent vein on the underside until it crested the head and slid through the moisture gathering there.

Elijah's breath caught, and the bite of teeth on Alex's collarbone sent a shiver up his spine like a line drive straight back to the pitcher—a shot so fast you can't think, you can only react.

Alex increased the speed of his strokes from base to tip and back again. When he reached down with his other hand and cupped Elijah's heavy balls, Elijah's head fell back, a moan of pleasure ripping from his throat.

Leaning in, Alex nipped and sucked his way up Elijah's neck, to the corner of his jaw—the first faint hints of stubble grazing Alex's lips like ultra-fine sandpaper—all the while stroking Elijah, bringing him closer and closer to the edge, if the way the man had started to pant was any indication.

"Faster," Elijah managed as he threaded an arm around

Alex's waist, his hands palming Alex's ass and giving him a squeeze.

Elijah pumped into Alex's hand, his hips gaining momentum as Alex jacked him off. Then Elijah's hips went erratic, and he buried his head in the crook of Alex's neck, his warm breath super heating Alex's skin.

"*Jesus Christ.*" Elijah took Alex's hand in one of his own, guiding Alex to the speed, grip, and length of stroke that he liked best. "Like that, babe."

Babe?

Elijah went stiff, his breathing ragged, rough, raw. Beneath Alex's hand, the spurt of Elijah's spunk came from deep down, the heat and slickness of semen spilling into their joined hands.

Elijah chuckled, his smile shy. "Damn." He pulled Alex in for a kiss, his tongue sweeping in. "That—"

"Cut!"

Alex brought Elijah back in for the kiss. Fuck. Were all guys this good at kissing or just Elijah? Alex couldn't get enough of that man's mouth. And those lips. "That was—"

"*Hot.*" Elijah finished for him.

Vin tapped Alex on the bicep with the back of his hand. "You guys can stop now. We're done filming."

"Yeah. Right. Sorry about that." Elijah's softening cock dropped from Alex's hand.

"Nice work, guys," Niko called out, his attention already going to Rose who had something on a laptop she needed to show him.

Sebastian moved onto the set, tossed Alex and Elijah a damp towel for a cursory clean up, and laid their robes on the couch behind them. "We've got one more shoot for the day, then Niko is taking everyone out to dinner."

"Sure," Alex said.

Elijah made one of those faces and Alex knew the next thing out of the man's mouth would be an excuse. "I've got this thing," he said, rather non-committally. "I'm gonna have to take a rain check."

"Sure, whatever. Niko likes to host a dinner to thank everyone for their hard work. It's not mandatory." Then he turned to Alex as he started backing off the set. "You'll be there, right?"

Alex had thought he would have wanted to get away as soon as he could from the guy who'd sucked his cock, but he felt strangely disappointed that Elijah wouldn't be there. He'd didn't want to go to dinner and be the only new guy, but he didn't have much of an excuse either. "I'll be there."

The two of them finished cleaning up as best they could with the damp towels, but as Alex shrugged into his robe, there was something niggling at him. "Hey, Eli…" He didn't know how to say what he had to say without it coming out wrong or sounding needy.

Elijah glanced around, but everyone had left the set. Only the two of them remained. He cocked his head and really focused on Alex.

"Hey, man. You got something to say, don't be shy about saying it to me. I know we don't know each other that well, but you had your dick in my mouth. I think that kind of forces openness, and intimacy, yeah?"

Alex huffed out a laugh. "I guess you have a point." Still…

Say it, scrote.

"It's… At the end there, you called me 'babe.'"

The stutter in the Elijah's movement as he tied his robe didn't escape Alex's attention. Though he wouldn't have noticed if he hadn't been watching Elijah's hands and avoiding looking him in the eye. "Did I?"

Alex shrugged. "It was probably—"

"An *in the moment* kind of thing. You know. Didn't mean anything."

"Yeah. Of course. I didn't think—I mean..." Alex scrubbed his hand down his face. He shouldn't have said anything. Embarrassment rushed in as if he'd stepped onto the mound for the first time and every pitch he threw landed three feet in front of the plate, the crowd roaring with laughter.

Elijah clapped him on the shoulder. "Come on. Time to hit those showers."

7

AN IN THE MOMENT *KIND OF THING*.

Alex grunted, pushing the plate on the incline leg press. It was his last set on his dreaded leg day. His quads burned, his legs shook, and he should be concentrating on his breathing, not on the words Elijah had said to him more than three weeks before.

"Four more." Trevor coached from beside him. They were at the gym attached to, and run by, the rehab facility. While this wasn't one of Alex's rehab sessions, for the past few months he and Trevor had started working out together after hours, pushing each other that extra mile or two.

"What?"

Trevor bumped his chin towards Alex. Alex glanced down at his legs. His knees were locked, the plate fully extended. He hadn't realized he'd stopped in the middle of his set. Jesus, he needed to get his head in the game before he hurt himself.

He flexed his knees and straightened them again as Trevor counted down the reps.

"Four. Three. Two."

Alex gritted his teeth, straining on the last rep. But Trevor egged him on.

"Come on, come on. Push, you pussy. One."

"Scrote," Alex said as he blew out a breath on his last rep. He'd need a wheelchair to make it out of the building because chances were, he'd never walk again.

"Scrote? What the hell are you talking about?"

"Scrotes are weak, pussies are—"

Trevor gave Alex his patented what-the-actual-fairy-fuck look.

"Never mind. Forget I said anything."

Sweat dripped down Alex's face, and Trevor tossed him a towel. "What's up with you, man? You've been weird these past few weeks and…"

Trevor's words died as one of the gym regulars came out of the locker room. Trevor clocked the gym rat all the way to the squat rack. "Damn, I'd give up a nut to spot for that man."

Alex watched the man as well. One of the many dedicated bodybuilders the high-end gym attracted. Trevor swatted Alex on the shoulder.

"What?"

"I'm gay. I've got an excuse for ogling that guy. What's your excuse?"

Alex swiped his keys and his water bottle off the mat. "I can appreciate a man's body without being gay. I can see the hard work he's put in, the dedication, the consistency, the sacrifice."

"Uh huh." Trevor's eyes narrowed, all in good fun.

But Alex had had about enough of this gay shit. Especially since it had been a constant narrative running non-stop through his head ever since he'd left Black Stallion. "Knock it the fuck off. Okay?"

Trevor held up his hands. "Sorry, dude." Why the hell was Trevor the one who looked offended?

"Look there's nothing wrong with being gay."

Trevor gave an exaggerated toss of his head and a snap of his fingers. A side of him he rarely showed. "Damn straight."

"But I'm not. Can you drop it?" Alex headed for the locker room. All he wanted was a shower and some food and a comfy bed so he could get up tomorrow and do it all the fuck over again. His own personal hellish version of *Groundhog Day*.

And probably do all that work for nothing. Because yeah, his career was on life support and he was too damn stubborn to reach over and pull the plug.

Trevor caught up to him and joined him in the locker room. "Why are you being so sensitive? You know I didn't mean anything by it."

Alex plopped down on the bench. His legs sighed with relief. "I know you didn't. Let's forget about it, okay? I'm tired and hungry and—"

Trevor looked him up and down. "Is that all it is?"

"Why wouldn't it be?"

Babe.

An in the moment *kind of thing.*

Gah! Alex needed a good solid wall to bang his head against and knock Elijah's voice out of his brain once and for all. Maybe one of the lockers would do.

Trevor stared at him, then his expression went soft, Alex knew he wasn't going to like whatever came out of his friend's mouth next. "Can I show you something in my office?"

Inside his locker, Alex's phone rang. "Hang on a sec." Alex opened his locker and picked up his cell phone. Frankie Chin. A reporter from the local news station. Alex had gone to high school with the guy. That was the only reason Alex could give to explain why Chin was so obsessed with Alex's rehab. Newsflash, his career was still in the shitter.

"You need to get that?"

Alex sent the call to voice mail and noticed three other missed calls. All from Chin, but no messages. The guy seriously needed to get a hobby. Or find another broken down athlete to stalk. "No. It's fine."

He returned his phone to the locker. "Give me ten minutes to shower. I'll meet you there."

The shower could have waited, but he needed a few minutes alone because, for some reason, unease sloshed around in Alex's gut making him feel... off. It wasn't so much what Trevor had said about wanting to show him something as much as it was the timidity in his voice and the way he'd looked past Alex when he'd said it. It rattled him.

"Sure. See you in ten."

Alex had the locker room to himself. He grabbed his towel and headed to the showers. The gym had a bank of individual stalls, and Alex stepped into the first one. He hung his towel on the hook and turned on the water, cranking up the heat to help loosen his tight muscles.

He'd rinsed off before he realized he'd left his shampoo and body wash in his locker. He stuck his hand under the dispenser on the wall and squirted the generic shampoo into his hand and started lathering his hair.

The shampoo was slow to suds and the smell... Alex closed his eyes and sniffed the suds in his hands. The aroma vaguely reminded him of sea and spice, like the shampoo in the showers back at Black Stallion.

Blood rushed south at the scent memory. Some sort of dickified Pavlovian response. Without bidding, and despite the mental blocks Alex had tried to erect in his brain since his little foray to Black Stallion, Elijah's handsome face popped into Alex's head.

Alex rinsed his hair and, lacking his body wash, used the

shampoo to lather up his body, his dick already hard by the time he got around to washing his junk.

You're not jacking off to Elijah.

Didn't stop you the last time. Or the time before that or the time—

Alex slapped his hand down on the shower control. *"Enough!"*

"You talking to me, dude?" someone said from around the corner.

Alex pinched the bridge of his nose. He'd been so up in his head he hadn't heard anyone come in. "No, man. Sorry."

After a perfunctory drying off, Alex wrapped the towel around his waist and strode back to his locker, beads of water dripping from his hair and down his chest and back.

The man gave Alex a bob of his chin. Alex returned it without a word. He'd seen the guy around before, but they'd never really spoken. For the first time since his more inhibited days in junior high, Alex slipped his underwear and jeans on under his towel. Alex would rather let the guy think he was shy than let a stranger see the wood he sported. Not that the guy was looking or anything.

Alex's phone rang again, but he silenced it and slipped it into his pocket without looking at the number. He finished dressing and shouldered his gym bag, heading for Trevor's office over at the rehab facility.

At Trevor's open door, he knocked.

Trevor glanced up from his computer. "Come in. Close the door."

"Now you've really got me scared."

Trevor rolled a pen across his knuckles and back again. "The recreational baseball signups are due at the end of the day. You're signing up on our team, right? We're a couple of men short."

"This is why you called me in here?"

"No, but my team captain is on my ass."

The last thing Alex wanted to do was play on a rec league like some has-been or forty-year-old man in therapy because he'd never been picked for the high school baseball team.

"I thought this was an all-gay team."

"They're willing to make an exception for you as long as you can hit the ball."

"I'm a pitcher. The Grizzlies didn't sign me because I could hit."

"Come on, man, you still hit better than most of them. Besides, as your physical therapist, I think it would be good for your arm for you to throw the ball around and not pitch."

"I do throw the ball around."

Trevor stared at him.

"Fine." Though it really wasn't. At least one of them was smiling. "Put me on the list. Now, tell me what I'm doing here."

Trevor's smile dropped, and the pen fell from his hand. "It could be nothing, but I didn't want it to turn into something and have it completely blindside you."

Alex plopped into the single seat across from Trevor's desk. Trevor's office was only big enough for the one visitor chair, so Trevor walked around and leaned against the front of the desk looking like he had bad news to break—like someone had keyed Alex's Challenger, or his dog had died.

Only, he didn't have a dog.

And his car was tucked safely away at his apartment since he'd run to the gym that day.

"Spit it out." Watch it be something stupid. Trevor *did* have the rare flare for the dramatic.

"Fine."

Trevor spun his laptop around and pressed play. Alex watched as he and Elijah came to life on a nineteen-inch screen in full retina display.

"*I'm coming.*" It was Alex's own voice. The sound card on the computer wasn't too shabby either. He could almost feel the scratch of the words as they'd tore out of his throat. He watched as 2D Elijah took him deep.

Alex had already relived that moment every night while he lay in bed, and driving down the street, and working out. Seeing Elijah go down on him as it rolled across the screen wouldn't help Alex get his mind right.

Jesus Christ. 3D Alex's dick pressed against his fly, and he reached out and slammed the lid down. He glanced over his shoulder at the door to make sure no one had seen, but Trevor's office door didn't have a window. "What the fuck, man. Why are you showing me this?"

"You never told me you decided to work for Black Stallion."

"And? Who are you? My mother?" Trevor had been his physical therapist from day one post-surgery. They'd spent a lot of time together. They'd become friends, good friends, but that didn't mean Trevor had the right to judge him. "What's the big deal? You're the genius who suggested I do it to begin with."

"I don't care that you did it—"

"Great." Alex stood, prepared to leave. "Now that I have your blessing, *Mom*, can I go?"

Not that he needed Trevor's permission to leave, or do porn, or do anything else in his life that Alex wanted to.

"What are you, sixteen? Sit your ass down." Trevor's jaw worked back and forth as if he were considering what he would say next. "Jesus, you're more of a queen than I am."

Alex plopped back down into the chair, and the seat cushion protested with a loud *ppffft*. He made a get-on-with-it-motion with his hand.

When Trevor had Alex's begrudging, if not full, attention, he said, "I didn't find your video on Black Stallion's website."

The unease that had sloshed around in Alex's gut earlier

turned into a whirlpool. He leaned forward in the chair, his hands gripping his knees. "What are you getting at?"

"I got the link in an email from a PT colleague who sent it to me and a few others in the pro athlete business."

"He likes gay porn, so what?"

Trevor gave him a slow, incredulous blink. "Were you in a corner jerking off while the powers that be passed out common sense?"

Trevor paused as if he expected a response. When Alex didn't give one, he continued. "He wasn't sharing the video because he liked it, he shared it because he was trying to figure out who you were. He wanted to know if any of us had a name to put with the dick." His tone had that *duh* quality to it Alex found so annoying.

"So?" God, he really did sound like a moody teenager. "They never show my face. Out of the millions of men in this country, I doubt they'll pull *my* name out of their asses. Besides, what difference does it make to them who some headless guy in a random porn is?"

"You don't get it, do you?"

Alex leaned back and raised his hands in defeat. "Clearly not."

"This guy noticed your scar from your Tommy John surgery. Saw your bee tattoo on your ribs. He wants to know who you are. He knows whoever it is would have had to have had PT after surgery and thought one of us might know who it was. The guy's a dick and has the tabloids on their favorite's list."

Alex's mouth went dry. He had to peel his tongue off the roof of his mouth to speak. "What did you tell him?"

Trevor grabbed both sides of his head. "Oh my God. What do you think I said?" But Trevor didn't give Alex a chance to answer. "I told him I had no fucking clue."

Alex closed his eyes and took one of those deep, calming

breaths he used to take on the mound. The ones he'd learned to take to decelerate his heart, to get his breathing under control to keep him from hyperventilating, but he could hear the rasp of his breath over the blood whooshing past his ears.

"Alex, look at me." When he did, Trevor said, "This day and age, it shouldn't be a big deal for a professional athlete to come out as gay—"

"I'm not gay." Alex was getting tired of saying it, especially when it seemed like Trevor never heard him. "You know Black Stallion makes their performers sign a contract stating they're straight, right?"

"*Perceived* as gay, then. Can you name any current and out gay pro baseball players? No? Me either."

"In the grand scheme of things, I'm a nobody."

"Trust me, brother, this video hits the tabloids, you'll become *somebody*. You need to lay low. Don't do any more shoots until this thing blows over. Or ever. The cash isn't worth it."

"Says the man cashing a paycheck every month and eating something besides Ramen noodles."

Even before the email, Alex had almost decided against going back to Black Stallion. He'd already spent too many hours with Elijah on his brain, wrestling with his sexuality, and trying to square who he'd thought he was with who he'd been that weekend.

All that angst and anxiety had spun him off his game, making him lose focus on winning an invite to spring training, that one tiny thread of his career that he clung to like a lifeline.

And he refused to let that go.

"Look, man, no judgment here. You do what you gotta do. I'm trying to watch your back is all."

"I appreciate it." Alex stood. He needed to get out of there, to process what Trevor had told him. There had to be some way to shut this down before it got out of hand. "We done here?"

"One more question."

"What is it?"

"How was he?" His low voice had that conspiratory tone to go along with the tell-me-everything smile.

Alex shoved his hands into his pockets. He wasn't smiling. "I'm not going there with you."

"Okay, fine. You don't kiss and tell. I can admire that. Just tell me, was he hung? He looks hung."

Trevor was such a cock hound. Despite everything, Alex chuckled. "Bye, Trevor."

————

"WHAT A SHIT SHOW." ELIJAH SAT AT A TABLE WITH DEMETRI Stavros, the art professor and now friend. He stared up at the big screen across the room as he nursed a beer in a dive bar a block off campus.

Saturday night and the bar was jam-packed—all the college kids getting drunk on cheap pitchers of beer and making fools of themselves as they tried to get laid—four weeks to the day since the last time Elijah had seen Alex.

Much longer than that since he'd been laid himself.

In the preceding weeks, Elijah hadn't been able to wipe Alex from his mind. Hell, he'd taken Shannon, the woman from the life drawing class, up on her offer of coffee a few times. She was a sweet girl but, in the end, he'd only been in it for the caffeine and the conversation.

Alex had been so stuck in Elijah's subconscious that when he'd decided he had to do something besides go to class and study and think about Alex, he'd gone to the campus rec center and amongst all the signups for fall rec leagues—racquetball, basketball, archery, rock climbing, co-ed volleyball—he'd signed up for the rec baseball team starting up the next week.

He hadn't played baseball since he'd aged out of little league.

And besides catching a World Series game on television every year or so, he'd thought little about the sport.

Until four weeks ago.

Freud might have had a few interesting things to say about that.

Now, his infatuation with Alex bordered on the obsessive. From trolling Google for old interviews and film clips and social media accounts, to jacking off at night imagining it was Alex's hands on his cock, not his own.

He really had to get a grip.

At a weak moment, at the risk of Niko finding out he was bi, he'd considered taking Demetri up on his previous offer at a chance to get to know him better.

Ultimately, it hadn't mattered how attractive the professor was, a friendship was all Elijah wanted from him. Elijah didn't want a dick attached to just any man, he wanted a specific man on the other end of that dick.

He wanted Alex.

On the TV screen, several reporters had cornered Alex as he left the San Fernando Sports Complex where many pro athletes worked out in the offseason. They shoved microphones in his face, throwing questions, demanding answers.

"How did anybody figure out it was him in the Black Stallion video?" Demetri asked. "I've seen it. Niko made sure his face never showed."

"You think the reporters are bad? Social media is blowing up. Rumors are flying—about someone recognizing his tattoo from a gay orgy, to a physical therapist who saw the scar on his elbow and somehow figured it out, to a girl he'd slept with who'd recognized him. I don't know what's true, if any of it is."

The news report went to a triple split screen. On the right: Alex as he tried to plow through the reporters to get to his car.

In the middle: a still shot of Alex's torso from the video—with Elijah's head in Alex's lap, thank you very much. On the left : a photo of Alex in a team locker room all sweaty after a game with his shirt stripped off. It had to have been from a couple of years ago. There was no visible scar on his elbow at that time, but the bee tattoo over his left ribcage was unique and damning.

"What about you," Demetri said. "Anyone recognize you?"

"Not yet, though I'm sure it's coming. Luckily, I'm unknown. Nobody really cares if I'm on video sucking a guy off."

On screen, Alex managed to get to his car, but as the reporters surrounded the vehicle, it was apparent Alex wasn't going anywhere until he answered some questions.

Someone at the table next to Elijah called out to the bartender. "Hey, man, turn it up."

The crowd also quieted down a bit. At least enough for Elijah to make out what the reporters were saying if he listened close enough.

"Alex, Alex." A female reporter elbowed to the front and shoved a microphone in Alex's face. "Do you deny that's you in the video?"

"Pretty hard to deny at this point." There were dark smudges under Alex's eyes that didn't have anything to do with having applied Eye Black to block the glare of the sun.

"I'd be so pissed," Demetri said.

Television Alex looked more resigned than angry.

"Aren't you embarrassed—" the reporter started.

Alex managed a cocky grin. It almost made it to his eyes. "I did a job—a damn good job if the video ratings are anything to go by. I get paid for my time. Same as you."

"But this was porn. *Gay* porn—"

"Trust me, lady, I'm *intimately* aware of that."

A round of laughter rumbled through the bar. Elijah and

Demetri knocked their glasses together in a silent toast. Elijah gave Alex points for owning his decisions.

"But I don't get—"

"No, lady, what *I* don't get is why you all care? Straight actors play gay roles all the time. Reporters weren't in Gyllenhaal's and Ledger's faces after they'd filmed *Brokeback Mountain* asking if they were gay. This is no different."

Another reporter squeezed his way in. He was lean and femme and, not that Elijah was judging, but if anyone on that screen was gay, it was that guy. "Are you straight?" The reporter wasn't afraid to come right out and ask the question on everybody's mind.

"Are you?" Alex countered.

"That's no one's business."

"*Exactly.*" The reporters fell silent a beat, then Alex said, "Here's what everyone needs to know." The patrons in the bar got quiet, and Alex took one of the reporter's microphones and held it to his mouth. "Gay or straight, my fastball breaks a hundred, my changeup is sick, and with training and hard work, my curve is getting nastier every day. When a pitch leaves my hand, the batter is going to have more to worry about than where I put my... *bleep.*"

The network bleeped it when Alex had said 'dick,' but it didn't take a genius to read his lips.

A cheer went up in the bar. From the gays and the straights. Gotta love a progressive college campus.

The news cut to commercial. Demetri laughed. "Fuck me, man. You've got yourself a winner."

Elijah tossed back the rest of his beer. "He's not mine. He's a guy I shot a scene with."

Demetri eyed him as he finished his beer as well, looking like he was about to call bullshit. But instead, he said, "You should give him a call. He could probably use a friend."

"I didn't get his number." Elijah still kicked himself about that one. But really, if he had, what would he have expected to happen? That they'd hang out? Go drinking at the bars? Play video games?

Hook up?

Then what, genius?

"I can get it from Niko if you'd like." Demetri sounded more like a matchmaker than a college professor.

Elijah wanted to say yes. But in his heart, he knew pursuing Alex would be stupid, even though Elijah couldn't get the guy out of his head. It was nothing more than a wishful infatuation brought on by some ball tingling kisses and a hella hot hand job.

All that aside, Elijah knew himself. He was attracted to men but preferred women for his romantic relationships. Whatever the hell was going on in Alex's head, Elijah didn't want to barge into his life and scramble him up and make him question his sexuality any more than he might already be doing now.

Especially if nothing could come of it.

And Elijah knew Alex had to be questioning. Elijah didn't care what anyone said. A man didn't kiss another man the way Alex had kissed him and not, on some level, have felt the attraction.

Besides, they couldn't risk doing anything that jeopardized negating their residuals clause on their contract with Black Stallion.

Neither one of them could afford that.

"No." Elijah was probably the last person Alex wanted to hear from. A twinge of regret pinched in the center of Elijah's chest. "I don't want his number."

8

On the mound, in the cages at the San Fernando Sports Complex, the SFSC, Alex could leave his jacked-up life and the stack of reporters—more persistent than a drug-resistant STI—outside.

The past week had been insane ever since the press had pushed his video with Black Stallion into the mainstream spotlight. He'd never gotten that much press, not when he'd been a first-round draft pick and not in the aftermath of injuring his elbow.

And the blowback from some of his friends had been equally distressing, to the point he'd stayed off social media and pretty much stopped answering texts and calls.

Though to be fair, the sizable residual check he'd received that morning from Black Stallion no doubt had something to do with all the downloads the video was getting from the free publicity.

The sex-negative media would make everyone believe that what he'd done was wrong, and the random people on the street that reporters had interviewed seemed to agree. But it was probably those same people who'd gone straight home and paid good money to watch Elijah go down on him.

No publicity is bad publicity.

Maybe. But whoever had said that hadn't been outed for being in gay porn. He didn't like how it had happened, but his wallet hadn't complained.

"Throw the heater again," Alex's pitching coach, Fernando Gomez, said from the other end of the cage. The two-time Cy-Young award winner looked like he could take the mound and win it all again even though he'd been retired for ten years.

Behind home plate, Alex's catcher buddy, Ethan Locke from the Hawks, squatted behind the plate, slapped his glove, then held it out as a target for Alex. "Bring it."

Behind Ethan and outside the cage, Gomez aimed the radar gun as Alex went into the windup. His arm hadn't felt this good since way before the surgery. If nothing else, the porn cash had given him the means to hire one of the best pitching coaches on the west coast. Plus a little extra to slip Ethan's way to compensate him for his time behind the plate, though Ethan would have done it for nothing.

And because of Trevor and Gomez and Ethan—and Black Stallion—for the first time since the Hawks had released him, Alex had reason to hope that his career may not be over.

In the past few weeks, Gomez had made slight adjustments to Alex's delivery and follow through that seemed to be making a difference on his speed, control, and spin rate.

Alex's lead foot landed on the slope of the mound, and he let the ball fly, taking care not to open his shoulders too soon or release his grip too late.

The ball landed in the web of Ethan's glove with a sharp *thwap.*

"*Jesucristo,*" Gomez had a self-satisfied smile on his face. "One-oh-three."

Ethan went to his knees and pushed up his mask—one of those hockey-style catcher's masks custom painted with the Hawks' signature silver and blue colors. "I can't wait to see those fuckers' faces at spring training when they see you throw."

Alex walked off the mound and caught the ball Ethan threw back. "If I score an invite."

"Kick that out of your mind," Gomez said. "I'm working on that. That's my job. Your one job is throwing the best pitch that you can, each time you step on that mound. That's the only thing you've got any control over."

Out of habit, Alex dug his foot next to the rubber, even though he was wearing his turf shoes instead of his spikes and the mounds in the complex's cages were covered in AstroTurf instead of Beam clay.

"One more pitch, then you're done for the day." Gomez put the radar down.

Alex flipped the tip of his glove toward Ethan, the sign he planned on throwing a curve ball. When he made the pitch, he twisted his wrist and gave it a snap, letting the ball roll off the end of his middle finger.

Out of his hand, the ball traveled much like his changeup, except for the spin he'd put on the ball. The last few feet before the ball crossed the plate, the bottom dropped out of it, and Ethan went to his knees to block the ball.

"Ho, man." Ethan tossed his mask to the side and stood. "That sucker was *sick*. If—"

Ethan cut himself off, but Alex knew what lay on the tip of his friend's tongue. *If you hadn't left that curveball hanging over the plate, the Hawks never would have let you go.*

Ethan met Alex halfway to the mound and shook his hand, bringing him in for a celebratory one-arm hug. "Thing of beauty, man. I should be paying you to let me catch."

"Thanks, man. It felt good."

Alex's phone rang, but he ignored it as he helped pick up a few scattered balls. Then it rang again. Ethan finished packing up his gear and gave Alex a wave as he left the cage. Gomez sat on a bucket of balls against a wall, engrossed in his own phone conversation.

As Alex reached for his phone, a sense of dread washed over him. Most of his friends had given up calling, but he hadn't heard from his parents. The news hadn't been pushed through to the national outlets and his parents lived across the country now, but there was no way the news hadn't gotten back to his father. His father was too plugged into the baseball scene not to have been told.

Or been given shit for it.

He should have called his parents when the story broke, but that hadn't been a call he'd looked forward to, so he'd put it off, then put it off some more. And now, more than a week out... well, he'd figured his dad would call him.

But he hadn't.

Which worried Alex even more.

Picking up his phone, Alex glanced at the call, but it wasn't a number he recognized. He almost sent it to voice mail, but screening calls and hiding out had proved tiring.

You can lie to everyone else, but don't lie to yourself.

Okay, so maybe there was that small part of him that secretly hoped the incoming call was Elijah reaching out. Not that Elijah owed him a thing, but it would have been nice to hear his voice.

"Hello," Alex said.

"Hey, it's Niko."

Alex blew out a disappointed breath and dropped down on his own bucket of balls.

"You there, kid?"

With an elbow on his knee, Alex rested his head in his hand. "I'm here."

"I'm sorry about what happened. We did our best—"

"None of that was your fault. I'm a big boy. I can take responsibility for my actions."

"How are you holding up?"

Alex didn't want to talk about it. Taking responsibility and talking about it when it had been the only thing in Alex's head —except for a borderline migraine—for the past week were two different things. Talking about it would only lead to cussing... or crying.

He changed the subject. "What can I do for you?"

Niko didn't miss a beat. "How about another scene?"

"Excuse me?" Alex's voice squeaked. He glanced around. Gomez wasn't paying him any attention, but he didn't want his conversation with his porn director overheard. "Hang on a sec."

For privacy, Alex climbed out of the cage, went around the corner, and walked to the end of a short hall next to a utility closet. "Say that again."

"Black Stallion wants you and Elijah to shoot another scene together. I know the publicity has brought you a lot of heat, but if you're smart, you can turn that to your advantage."

"And yours."

"And mine." Niko didn't seem put out by Alex's rudeness or the blatant accusation that Niko was only in it for the money. Which, it was Niko's business, so really what other reason would Niko have? "The on-screen chemistry you two share is off the charts. I saw it. More importantly, the viewers saw it. Even before this thing blew up in your face. Might as well make a profit from the mess."

"I might hold out for the book deal."

Niko laughed. It was short and sharp. "I like your attitude."

"When?"

"Friday. The scene will be longer, more involved, but that means more cash up front as well."

That was only four days away. And one of his training days with Gomez. He'd have to check with Gomez and Ethan to see if they could switch their schedule.

But Alex didn't have to pull up his banking app to know how astronomically fast his rehab, coaching, and cage rental fees were draining his funds. And after how well he'd pitched today, he couldn't afford to slack off now.

"I need the money. I'll be there." His stomach lightened, and his heart rate bumped up a notch at his decision.

You need the money. That voice inside his head nearly dropped to its knees against his brainpan, and laughed.

Money's not the reason you said yes. You didn't ask for details. What does 'longer' and 'more involved' mean?

The reason you said yes was six feet of muscle with a dick you can't wait to get your hands on again.

The semi Alex now sported beneath his athletic shorts made it hard for him to argue against himself.

Gomez popped his head around the corner. "Hey, I'm headed out. See you Friday."

Alex jogged down the hall after his pitching coach. "About Friday..."

––––––––

SINCE ALEX'S SCENE WITH ELIJAH WASN'T SCHEDULED UNTIL midday on Friday after Darius, Grant, and Reyes shot a scene, Alex had opted to drive to the studio that morning instead of spending the night.

Now, he sat alone in his robe on a leather couch along the back wall of the Ready room with his hair and makeup done with only thirty minutes before their scheduled shoot time.

Alex's leg bounced, and his attention span was too short to

read a hundred and forty characters on social media. Where the hell was Elijah? He should have been there an hour ago.

Was he okay?

Or had he backed out?

A knock came at the door, and Alex glanced up, expecting to see Elijah, but it was only Sebastian and some other performer Alex had been introduced to earlier, Chet or Charlie or something like that. Alex hadn't bothered to remember, he'd had Elijah on his mind.

The kid looked like he was fresh off the cattle car from Texas, dressed in his Wranglers, boots, western shirt, and a black cowboy hat. Complete with the over-sized silver belt buckle. Alex could practically smell the sage and shit wafting off him.

"Anyone heard from Elijah?" Alex went for a deceptively casual tone, but his tension made his pitch off.

"Yeah, he called not too long ago. Apparently, he had a test this morning that ran late. He's on his way but hit a snag on the I-5. Niko said that if he's not here in ten minutes, we're going to have to shoot the scene without him."

Alex bit back an emphatic curse, along with his urge to throw his clothes back on and walk out the door. Instead, he sat there with that sinking feeling as if a heavy weight had been strapped around his ankle and he'd been thrown into quicksand. If he hadn't already signed on the dotted line that morning, he would have considered backing out. "Another solo scene then?"

He hated to give some of the cash back that Niko had handed him because no way a solo scene would pay as well as one with Elijah.

"Oh, no. If Elijah doesn't get here, you'll be doing your scene with Chet." The smile on Sebastian's face said, *See? Crisis averted.*

Chet stepped out from behind Sebastian and pushed his hat up onto his forehead. He was short and muscular with a thick neck and arms. He looked like he wrestled steers and hauled bales of hay by hand just for kicks. No doubt Black Stallion's customers would wanna get their rocks off to that piece of fresh, farm meat.

Too bad Alex didn't.

That weight around Alex's ankle doubled, and his chest got tight as if he'd sunk up to his chin in the quicksand. He didn't want to do a scene with Chet. Contract or no contract, Alex had to say something. "Sebastian, can I talk to you a minute? In private?"

Sebastian took a step back, and Alex wanted to reach out and grab his hand to keep him from going. "I really need to get back to the set. Can it wait? Things are crazy this morning. Nothing seems to be going right."

You can say that again.

"If I could have a second with Niko, I—"

He could what? Fuck. He couldn't back out. Not only did he need the money, but that contract he'd signed had never specified who his scene partner would be. The only thing Alex had was a verbal agreement from Niko that his partner would be Elijah.

From down the hall, Cat called out a greeting. They all turned to the door. Elijah popped his head in, looking frazzled with his eyes wide and hair messy. "Sorry I'm late. Cat said it shouldn't take her long to get me ready."

Alex didn't have time to greet Elijah before he disappeared again. But there would be plenty of time for that later. Elijah was here, and Alex didn't have to do a scene with the country boy, that was all that mattered.

"You were saying?" Sebastian prompted.

Alex waved his hand dismissively and spared a smile for Chet. "Never mind."

Ditching and robe and dressing for the scene, Alex breathed

a little easier as if someone had thrown him a lifeline and dragged his ass out of the quicksand to safety.

No, not *someone*.

Elijah.

———

THIS TIME, BLACK STALLION USED THE MIDDLE SET FOR ELIJAH and Alex's scene, which had been staged to look like an office in a high-rise building. Complete with a sturdy desk, a matching white leather club chair and sofa, and a floor to ceiling window looking down over the New York skyline at night. It appeared so real Elijah had to walk over and touch the dummy window.

Sebastian placed a bottle of lube on a hidden shelf on the backside of the couch out of view of the cameras for easy access if needed. Then he stepped up beside Elijah at the window. "That view gave me vertigo the first time I walked on this set."

"Does he always make his sets look so real? I mean that garage set Grant and the rest of them used the last time I was here made me want to bring my truck in for repairs, and there's nothing wrong with it."

"One thing you'll learn about my uncle, he refuses to skimp on set design."

"Everyone ready?" Niko called out. He glanced around. "Now where the hell is Alex?"

"Here." Alex jogged around the corner from the hallway, his dress shoes slapping on the polished concrete. "Sorry," he said as he adjusted the knot on his suit tie. "Cat had to help me with this thing. I haven't had to wear a tie since the Grizzlies drafted me."

Elijah stood there, drinking Alex in like a thirsty man who'd walked through the Gobi Desert and back again. These weeks they'd been apart had made Elijah reach for his phone more than once with the intention of calling Demetri to get him Alex's number. When Niko had called Elijah up, asking if he wanted to do another scene with Alex, he hadn't hesitated.

If nothing else, Alex knew how to fill out a suit. Much like the set design, Niko hadn't skimped on the apparel either. That suit couldn't be bought at a box or department store.

That was the kind of suit that could almost fund a semester at Elijah's college.

Elijah had to avert his gaze before he tented his own suit pants. Unlike Alex who was all buttoned up, Elijah wore a dress shirt with the tie loosened, the sleeves rolled halfway up his forearms as if he were at the end of a long work day.

Which was part of the scenario Niko had spun out for Elijah and Alex: after hours at the office. Boss versus underling. The quintessential unequal power dynamic.

Near the back of the studio, Reyes, Darius, and some new cowboy dude pulled up director's chairs and sat to watch. There was no sign of Grant, though Elijah had been told he was also back shooting that day.

"Alex, you'll start offstage. When I say 'action,' you come through the door and let the scene play out the way we talked about earlier, clear?"

"Got it."

Vin moved closer, shouldering his camera. "Are we shooting Alex from the neck down?"

"No. You can show my face," Alex said. "That cat has already scratched and clawed its way out of the bag."

Vin gave him a thumbs up. "Fine with me. Makes my life easier."

Alex disappeared behind the set. Elijah had been running so late, he had hardly had the chance to say two words to Alex, besides what needed to be said for clarification for their scene.

He'd wanted to ask Alex how he was doing after the media

blow up and to apologize for not giving him a call. Not contacting him had been a dick move on his part.

Vin came forward with the camera, and Niko stepped back. "Elijah, we'll start with you behind the desk."

As Elijah took his position, Sebastian came around the corner with a phone, his free hand covering up the mouthpiece.

Niko frowned. "What now, Bass?"

Sebastian's nose scrunched up. "It's Peter."

"Jesus Christ," Niko muttered. "What is it now?"

The shrug said either Sebastian didn't know, or he didn't want to say. Elijah figured being put in the messenger position between Niko and his boyfriend would be awkward. "He says it's urgent."

"That's what he said the last time. And the time before that, and the time before that." Niko's voice rose with each word.

"You're going to give yourself a coronary," Sebastian warned.

Niko took a deep breath and then another, pinching the bridge of his nose.

"You want me to tell him you'll call back after you're done filming?"

"Yeah. We've been through this. He knows not to call me during the day."

Sebastian walked off, speaking to Peter on the phone as he went, his voice velvet-smooth and cajoling.

Settling into his director's chair, and to no one and everyone, Niko said, "Anyone who says age is just a number, is a liar." Then to Vin, "You're the one who told me that a twenty-year age gap wasn't a big deal."

"I've got to deal this to you straight, boss. The age gap isn't the issue. Maturity is the issue. Peter is pretty, but he doesn't have much to offer you besides smooth skin and a hard dick."

Elijah waited for Niko to bark or bite, but instead, Niko

threw back his head and laughed, clapping Vin on the back. "Touché."

Then to everyone, Niko said, "Places, people."

Darius whistled from the shadows, and Reyes cupped his hands around his mouth and hollered out, "Show us what you've got! No pressure, baby!"

Niko turned in his seat. "You boys beat it."

"Awh, c'mon, man," Darius grumbled, but he, Reyes, and the cowboy headed out.

Niko sat and wrapped a foot around the bottom rung of the director's chair. "Action."

9

———————

WAITING FOR NIKO'S CUE, ALEX STOOD IN THE NEAR DARKNESS behind the set, his nerves jangling, dangling, pinging, and ponging. He shifted from foot to foot and shook out his arms trying to dispel the nervous energy.

As much as he wanted to get his hands on Elijah again, this scene would push and shove his comfort zone into a tight corner, his adrenaline already drip, drip, dripping, sending him into that fight or flight mode.

Don't. Scrote. Out.

Don't scrote out. Don't scrote out.

Don't scrote out, don't scrote out, don't scrote out.

Alex stuck a finger in the collar of his shirt and tugged. He couldn't get any air. What the hell was taking Niko so long?

He turned to walk back around the set and see what the hold up was when Niko call out 'action.'

Alex put his hand on the doorknob, closed his eyes and took that heart-calming deep breath.

As his heart slowed and his mind cleared, the raging hard-on in his pants reminded him not only could he *do* this, he *wanted* this. He blew the breath out.

Niko had given him one line of dialog to deliver and wanted him and Elijah to ad-lib from there. Niko had given Elijah more instructions that Alex hadn't been privy to, but Niko had told Alex to go with it. All the while reminding Alex they wouldn't breach the terms of the contract as far as what acts they'd agreed to, and that they could stop the scene at any time if they grew uncomfortable.

Frankly, it sounded like a disaster move leaving so much of how the scene would go up to a couple of noobs, but Alex wasn't the director, Niko was.

Niko called out 'action' again, and Alex walked through the office door. "You wanted to see me, boss?"

There. His one line, and he didn't mess it up.

Elijah ran his hand down his red silk power tie and stood. That same wolfish, predatory smile from that first weekend had landed on his face again. Alex couldn't tell if Elijah was acting or if the smile was real. "Close the door."

Alex did as he was told. When he turned back around, Elijah was leaning against the front of his desk, his hands gripping the edges. With Elijah's legs crossed at the ankles, the thin material of his dress pants couldn't hide his erection.

Alex stuck his finger in his collar again, the sweat starting to bead along his hairline.

Damn, those stage lights are hot.

His brain whirred, thinking up what to say next as he stepped farther into the office. "Was there a problem with the reports, sir?"

"No problem."

Think. Think. Think "If it's about the overtime, I—"

Elijah stood and closed the gap between them, stopping well inside Alex's personal space.

"I don't have a problem compensating you for your time." Elijah's voice dropped, gruff and ruff with innuendo that made

Alex's balls draw up and his spit evaporate. "I called you in here to give you your bonus."

Damn, Elijah was *gooood*.

"I... um... I mean..." One look in those eyes and whatever inane thing Alex had thought of to say vanished. His mind... *fucking blank.*

Where was his catcher to give him the signs? Could he call 'time' and have a mound visit?

Any second now, Niko would say 'cut,' if Alex didn't get his shit together. With the camera, Vin edged closer and closer.

Ignore the camera. Focus on Elijah.

Alex started, "About that bonus..."

Elijah fisted Alex's tie and grinned. "Don't worry about the rumors of underpayment." Elijah pushed Alex back, step by step until the cold glass of the window pressed against his back. "You're going to get what's coming to you."

The way Elijah's voice dipped, low and slow and deliberate with that edge of dominance cutting through—*Jesus Christ*—had the pre-cum dampening Alex's jock.

Then Elijah's mouth crashed into his. Not the timid taste of that first night. Elijah was all tongue and teeth and nips and sin. It took Alex aback for the briefest of seconds before he returned Elijah's kiss.

God, he'd missed those lips.

Alex tasted the mint on Elijah's tongue, smelled the clean scent of soap on his heated skin. Angling his head, Elijah took the kiss deeper, while his hands tore at the knot in Alex's tie.

The buttons popped on Alex's collar, and Elijah pulled the tie over Alex's head, then dove back into the kiss. With his eyes closed, Alex sensed more than saw Vin move closer with the camera. They had yet to hear any direction from Niko, so they kept going.

Elijah shifted, his muscled thigh going between Alex's legs

and pressing against his crotch. It was all Alex could do not to grind against it.

Why are you fighting it? Because you're afraid for anyone to know you like it?

Maybe.

It's a fucking porn shoot, you're being paid to look like you want it.

Damn straight.

Alex thrust against Elijah's leg, ripping a guttural groan from the back of Elijah's throat that made it impossible for Alex to keep his damn hands to himself. With speed and a focused determination, he worked his way down the buttons on Elijah's shirt as Elijah kissed and sucked his way down Alex's neck. One of Elijah's hands slid around and squeezed Alex's ass.

As soon as all the buttons on Elijah's shirt were undone, Elijah broke the kiss and stripped it off, tossing it away. Alex blew out a breath. He'd forgotten how beautiful the man was.

"Like what you see?"

Elijah was built more compact, his muscles more dense than Alex—his pecs, thick slabs of muscle, his abs cut with a thin trail of hair leading from the bottom of his belly button down beneath the waistband of his pants.

"I like." Alex wanted to touch, to feel, to—

Elijah swatted Alex's hand away. "Ah, ah, ah. This is your bonus, not mine."

Then Elijah grabbed each side of Alex's shirt and pulled. The buttons went popping and flying. One of them *plinked* as it bounced off the lens of the camera. Elijah yanked the shirt off Alex's shoulders and down his forearms, but the buttons at the cuffs remained fastened, effectively handcuffing Alex.

As he struggled to free himself, Elijah put his large hand on the center of Alex's sternum and pushed him back against the window. "Relax. It's my turn to repay all the hard work."

Alex had never dallied with any type of bondage, and as

bondage went, having his hands cuffed by a shirt was probably basic level kink, but *damn*...

With his arms trapped behind him, it made his chest bow out, more on display than he'd ever been in a stadium full of screaming fans. His jockstrap shrunk a size, and all Alex wanted to do was pull his cock free and find relief.

He glanced down at Elijah who had a wicked, wicked grin on his face. The man knew what effect he was having on Alex. Slowly, Elijah trailed his hand down Alex's chest. Goosebumps exploded, and sweat broke out into a glistening sheen on his skin.

Elijah edged closer, his erection pressing against Alex's hip as he licked and nibbled on Alex's earlobe. "Tell me what you want," Elijah whispered, but it was more than a whisper because it had to be loud enough for the mics to pick up.

Even though others watched, Elijah's words sounded close and intimate, and Alex imagined the two of them, alone, and with all the time in the world to explore each other's bodies, to find what brought them both pleasure and satisfaction.

Elijah tugged Alex's belt free and with a twist of his wrist, undid the clasp on Alex's slacks, the zipper easily sliding down as Elijah pulled the two halves of Alex's fly apart.

Alex flexed his hips, aching for Elijah's touch. With a nip to Alex's chin, Elijah said, "You want my hand on your cock?"

Alex's head fell back, thumping against the glass, and his breathing picked up. The muscles in his shoulders pulled and ached from having his arms restrained, but it was a good kind of pain. The kind of pain that had him squirming and straining for a different type of release.

Yeah, he wanted Elijah's hand on his cock, but the words refused to come. Alex nodded.

"Use your words," Elijah said, his fingers ghosting across

Alex's lower abdomen at the waistband of his *King Dong* jockstrap.

Elijah pulled far enough away to look at Alex's face. Elijah's pupils were almost blown, and his breaths became rushed and shallow. He was as affected as Alex, which made Alex feel emboldened.

"I want you to grab my cock."

Devilment played in Elijah's eyes as his hand slipped beneath the waistband of Alex's jock, those thick, strong fingers reaching down and cupping his balls.

Alex's head fell back with another bang against the glass, the thump radiating around his skull as he ground against Elijah's hand. Then Elijah's hot, wet mouth landed on Alex's nipple, and he couldn't swallow down the moan. Elijah's tongue tortured his nipple as Elijah took hold of Alex's shaft and began stroking.

So. Much. *Need*.

Alex struggled against his fabric handcuffs, needing to touch, to control, to sate. As much as he enjoyed Elijah's manhandling, there was something to be said for active participation.

Pre-cum leaked from Alex like a faucet with a faulty washer, his balls sucked up tight against his body. Fluid liberally coated Elijah's hand as Elijah worked his palm and fingers over the head of Alex's cock, his grip firm and strong.

"Both of you lose the pants and the jocks," Niko said from off set.

The words jarred and pulled Alex out of the moment, but he toed out of his shoes and Elijah stripped off his own clothes, kneeling to pull off Alex's pants.

At his feet, Elijah raked his gaze up Alex's body, inch by inch, past the tremble in his thighs, past the jutting of his erection, past the quiver in his belly, past the tumble of his heart in his chest, until their eyes met. Niko, Vin, the set, the lights... disappeared.

Alex couldn't take the sweet torture any longer. He lowered his voice, not caring if the mics picked up his words. "Free me."

Elijah stood, pressing his body against Alex's, thigh to thigh, pelvis to pelvis, cock to good-god-glorious cock.

Elijah didn't have Alex beat on length, but he had Alex on girth.

Sweat trickled down Alex's chest as Elijah reached around and manipulated the buttons on the shirt cuffs. As soon as Alex's hands were free, he put them on Elijah's shoulders and turned, shoving Elijah back against the window. The set rattled, Elijah's breath caught, and his eyes went wide a fraction before a bring-it-on grin creased his face.

Vin swung into a better position, catching Alex's eye, but as Alex rubbed his body up against Elijah's, their pre-cum mixing on their bellies, all Alex wanted was to put his mouth on Elijah.

Which wasn't in the script.

Alex didn't think too hard about what that meant.

He went where his desires led.

Elijah's arms wrapped around Alex's head, pulling Alex into the crook of his neck. Alex scraped his teeth along the tender skin, a shudder running through Elijah's body.

In Elijah's ear, Alex said, "I want to suck you off."

This hadn't been part of Niko's plan and Alex wanted to make sure Elijah was good with it. If Niko heard, if he had any objections to the change in plans, he didn't say anything.

Elijah thumped his head against the window twice, the cords in his neck straining, his throat working, trying to form words. Elijah grunted his consent, and as Alex licked and sucked his way down Elijah's torso, Elijah didn't stop him.

Dropping to his knees, Alex became aware of Vin going down on his own to get the best camera angle. Somewhere in the back of his mind, he thought Niko said, "go with it," but that could have been his imagination. Alex skimmed his fingers through the neatly trimmed mat of hair surrounding Elijah's cock before gripping the base.

Elijah strained in Alex's hand. So hard and thick. Alex looked up, past the drop of pre-cum on Elijah's tip to his scene mate's hooded, heated gaze.

Alex stuck his tongue out and licked the drop from Elijah's slit. The taste of salt made his own dick drip. Elijah's head fell back, a groan tearing from his lips as his fingers tangled in Alex's hair.

Then Alex took Elijah deep, and the man shuddered and pulsed in Alex's mouth.

"Ahh, *fuuuck*." Elijah's hand went to the back of Alex's head as he thrust deeper down his throat.

Using his hands, his mouth, his lips, his tongue, Alex worked and worked, bringing Elijah to the ragged edge. Alex's own balls lay heavy and in dire need of relief.

"Like that, babe," Elijah muttered between harsh pants. "Suck that cock."

Alex sucked him faster and harder, Elijah's cock hitting the back of his throat and threatening to make him gag, but he refused to stop.

"I'm coming," Elijah ground out as he tried to pull Alex off, but Alex wasn't having it.

He took Elijah deep, once, twice more before Elijah stiffened, and the pulse of Elijah's cum against Alex's fingers at Elijah's base arrived a second before he tasted the spunk on his tongue. He sucked and swallowed, Elijah's moans of pleasure making his own dick throb.

Then Elijah sank against the window, pulling Alex up off his knees. Alex's hand went to his dick and started pumping furiously, but Elijah knocked his hand away and took over.

With one arm around Elijah's neck, Alex pulled him in tight, their bodies sweaty and slick, the scent of sex heavy in the air, and the taste of Elijah on his tongue.

As aroused as Alex was, it wasn't going to take much to make him come. Alex thrust into Elijah's hand as Elijah stroked over the head again and again. The base of Alex's spine tingled, and his body shook as the climax short circuited his system.

Alex sank against Elijah as he milked him dry, Alex's breath hot, his lungs billowing. He pressed his forehead against Elijah's not caring who was watching or listening. "I hope that was okay."

"Jesus Christ." Elijah chuckled, as he caught his breath. That should have been the end. Niko should have called cut, but with a hand to the back of his neck, Elijah pulled Alex in for one last kiss. This one sweet and tender. "Yeah, that was more than okay."

"And cut!"

————

ELIJAH SHRUGGED INTO THE ROBE SEBASTIAN BROUGHT HIM AND started walking off the set when all he wanted to do was pull Alex aside and do what they'd done all over again, but this time without the cameras and the captive audience.

In the weeks since their first scene, their connection and chemistry had only intensified. He figured all that time apart with nothing to think about but when you might get your hands on each other again, kind of did that to you.

If Alex was interested in seeing him outside of Black Stallion, he wanted to make sure Alex didn't leave without getting his number.

Darius came skipping down the hall and around the corner riding an invisible stick pony and swinging a lariat, the fresh-from-the-farm kid not far behind him. "Come on, cowboy, let Darius take your sweet white ass for a ride."

Alex gave Elijah a nudge. "This should be worth sticking around for."

Elijah chuckled. "No kidding."

"You can't go back there. Peter. *Peter.*" Rose's heels *clackity clack clacked* on the concrete floors.

A man who Elijah assumed was Peter, brushed past Darius and the new guy with Rose running after him.

"I'm sorry, Niko," Rose said, "I tried to stop him."

"It's okay, Rose—"

"No, Rose, it's not okay. *Nothing* is okay." Peter's flushed face made him look like he'd been drinking, but Elijah didn't detect any slurring beneath the rage.

"Peter." Niko's voice remained calm and patient the way a parent's does when their toddler is pitching a fit in the middle of the toy store. "This isn't the right time or place."

"According to you, there is *never* a right time or place. So, I'm making it here. Now." Peter couldn't have been older than his mid twenties, though he'd clearly perfected teen drama.

Niko removed his reading glasses and set them and his clipboard aside. "The studio is my first priority. I made that clear from the start."

His voice ratcheting up with each sentence, Niko said, "How do you think I can afford the house, the car, the trips, and all the toys you like, if I don't work?"

Peter gaped at Niko, the truth a *smack-smack* to the face.

After a calming breath, Niko lowered his voice. "I never made you any promises."

"You want me to get rid of him, boss?" Vin stepped forward and clasped a hand around Peter's bicep.

Peter shoved Vin away and got in Niko's face. He was slender, slight, femme. And very pretty for a man. "Which one of them are you fucking, because you certainly aren't fucking me."

Niko patted the air with his hands in a calm-the-fuck-down kind of way. "Let's go to my office."

"I'll take him, boss."

Peter took a step back but didn't turn to leave. Elijah started to wonder if it would take all of them working together to get Peter out of the building.

"Is it him?" Peter pointed an accusatory finger at Vin. "It's him, isn't it? You two spend an awful lot of late nights here. Filming. Editing. Is that all you do? He's your type. Young and—"

"It's not like that. He works for me. I pulled him off the streets for crying out loud."

"To fuck."

"*No*, not to fuck. Peter, listen to me. I don't shit where I work. He means nothing—" Niko cut himself off and closed his eyes for a second when it hit him what he'd said.

"Jesus Christ." He turned his attention to Vin and said, "I didn't mean that the way it sounded, I—"

"I know what you meant, boss." Vin's voice didn't crack, and his expression didn't change, but Vin appeared to shrink before Elijah's eyes.

"You've completely lost your mind, Peter. I've had enough. It's over."

Peter laughed, one of those nervous laughs comedians have when they're the only ones laughing at their jokes. "Hard for something to be over when you were never in it to begin with."

"I think you need to leave. Vin, will you show—" Niko glanced around. "Where did Vin go?"

Elijah looked at Alex. Alex looked at Darius. Darius looked at Sebastian and Rose. They all looked around.

"I never saw him leave," Rose said.

"That cat split." Darius made a *vroot* sound, like fabric

ripping. "Someone accused me of sleeping with the boss, and I'd skate too, man. No offense, Niko."

"It's okay. I'll find him." Niko held his hand out toward the hallway. A silent invitation for Peter to leave. "Come on, Peter. I'll show you out."

After the two men left, Darius said, "That was *aaawkwaaard.* Am I right?"

Sebastian rolled his eyes and walked away.

"What?" Darius raised his arms out to the side. "I'm saying what everyone else is thinking. Don't be getting your pink panties in a twist."

Without turning around, Sebastian raised one hand and gave Darius the finger.

"Hey, man," Darius called out. "Name the time and the place."

Grant walked into the studio and bopped Darius upside the head and grumbled, "Knock it the fuck off."

"Ow." Darius backed toward the refreshment table along the rear wall. "I didn't mean nothin' by it."

The cowboy rocked back and forth on his heels, apparently at a loss for words.

Elijah shook Grant's hand, a simultaneous greeting, and goodbye. "I'm hitting the showers. I'll see you guys around."

"Same here." Alex bumped his chin in Chet and Grant's direction.

Elijah and Alex showered and dressed in silence, both lost in their own heads. He didn't know what Alex was thinking, but personally, he couldn't get the memory of Alex sucking him off out of his mind.

And while Alex had asked permission, and Elijah had not only climbed on board but rang the damn bell, he wasn't leaving without letting Alex know how he felt.

"So," Elijah finished tying his shoes and stood, "about that blow job..."

At the bank of lockers, Alex packed his dirty clothes into a gym bag with his back to Elijah. When he turned, he had a timid, I-really-don't-want-to-hear-the-truth smile on his face, the red creeping up his neck. "That bad?"

Elijah chuckled. "That good."

Alex tossed the bag on the bench, closed the locker door, and leaned back against it. Elijah glanced over his shoulder. There wasn't a lock on the door to the communal showers, but from where they stood, and because of the way the door swung, they'd have a few seconds' warning if anyone came in.

"I shouldn't have changed what we'd agreed on," Alex started, "that was a bullshit move, but with all the ad-libbing, I wanted... I thought..." Alex let the rest of the sentence drop.

"You wanna know what *I* thought?"

Alex's chuckle came out low and self-deprecating. "I don't know, do I?" Damn. Vulnerable Alex was adorable.

Elijah stepped closer, straddling Alex's leg. "I thought you gave fucking amazing head. You sure you've never sucked a guy off before?"

"Positive. I know what I like and hoped you'd like it, too."

"I did. Very much so."

Alex looked away. It had thrilled Elijah that Alex had taken the initiative. It was one thing to sit back on a couch and let a guy suck your dick. After all, you can close your eyes and pretend it's some hot, buxom, blonde, but taking that next step, getting on your knees and going down on another guy, makes it hard to pretend the person you are with is a woman.

What was it about this man that had Elijah questioning everything he thought he knew about himself? That hetero-romantic bi label he'd slapped on himself had started to itch and chafe and he wondered if Alex's label grated as well.

Elijah dropped his voice. "Look at me." When Alex did, Elijah said, "I was in a bar when your interview came up on the television."

"Oh God. What a cluster. I'm embarrassed you and everyone else had to see that."

"Embarrassed? You sat those fuckers down. You didn't grovel. You didn't apologize. You *owned* it. You owned *them*. I don't think I've ever been prouder of another person in my life."

Red rimmed Alex's eyes, and moisture gathered at the corners. Alex cleared his throat. "Thanks."

When Alex broke eye contact, Elijah cupped his cheek and turned Alex's face back to his. "When that shit blew up... I should have called, but—"

"You didn't have my number."

"I didn't. I could have gotten it, though. I wasn't sure you wanted to hear from me. But that's no excuse. I should have been there and offered you moral support. I'm apologizing for that."

Alex swallowed hard but didn't say anything, only nodded, pressing his forehead into Elijah's. They stood there like that, soaking up the skin-to-skin contact.

Elijah whispered, "I really want to kiss you. Yeah?"

Sucking in a breath, Alex said, "Yeah."

Elijah shifted, his erection brushing against Alex's hip and Elijah bit back the groan and forced himself not to grind against Alex. This wasn't about getting off.

This was about connecting.

He pressed his lips against Alex's. Once, twice, before going back for more, their tongues exploring, tasting as they breathed each other in.

If all Elijah wanted was to sleep with a guy and explore more of his bi side, he could do that anywhere. After all, dick was a lot easier to get than pussy. And while he didn't know exactly what he wanted, he knew he didn't want something random.

As a rule, Elijah hadn't been interested in relationships with men. But *this* man...? Perhaps Alex could prove the exception.

Angling his head, Alex took the kiss deeper, his hands threading through Elijah's damp hair and pulling him closer. Elijah's watch beeped, and he pulled away, his chest rising and falling as he caught his breath.

"I've got a study group session I have to get to."

"Yeah." Alex looked dazed and well-kissed. "Sure."

Elijah stepped away and gathered his own bag. He turned to leave, but didn't. Instead, he held out his hand and said, "Give me your phone."

Alex retrieved his phone from his pocket, unlocked the screen, and handed it over. Elijah punched in his name and phone number and handed it back. Was he really going to do this?

"I don't want to pressure you into anything you don't want to do. I'm going to leave the next move up to you. I'd like to see you again. Call if you feel the same."

10

Alex turned up at the Los Angeles County Sports Park twenty minutes early. Not that he was that eager to play baseball for Trevor's rec team, but he'd needed to get out of his apartment and get some air.

Hiding out from the press got old. Fast.

It had been ten days since he'd shot the office scene with Elijah. Luckily, when the video hit the website, the controversy and uproar weren't as bad. Though he had the occasional reporter show up at the oddest of places and shove a microphone in his face, looking for comments.

When he walked up to the field, he realized he wasn't alone. Sitting on the top row of the bleachers was one of the more persistent sports reporters.

He dropped his equipment bag against the backstop and raised his hand to her when she went to get up. "Don't."

She sat back down. "I'm doing my job, Mr. Payne."

"Aren't you sick of this yet? Wouldn't you rather be covering football or basketball or hell, anything that doesn't have to do with my dick?"

"You make news, we come around. That's how this works."

The woman stood. "Look, I'm supposed to meet my husband for dinner at seven. I'll make you a deal. Answer one question and then we both can get on with our lives."

At this point, he'd do about anything for a few hours without having to police his every move and every word around reporters. "Shoot."

"Are you doing gay porn as some sort of publicity stunt to stay forefront in the clubs' minds to try to get an invite to spring training?"

"You give me far too much credit. If I wanted to stay on the clubs' radar, I probably could have thought of a less career-damaging way to do it."

"Fair enough," the lady said as she put her notebook in her purse and stepped down from the bleachers. By the dugout, she turned and asked, "Who's Elijah Maddox?"

She posed the question as a throwaway, an afterthought. It landed like a well-calculated, well-researched blow between the eyes.

Alex's heart stopped for a beat, long enough for him to hear the anger bubbling and brewing in his brain. He'd known it would only be a matter of time before someone found out Elijah's name. Though he hadn't expected it so soon. He had to steel his voice and his expression so she wouldn't know how much the question had affected him.

"You've had your one question. Don't keep your husband waiting."

The lady slid her sunglasses onto her smug face. "Have a good evening, Mr. Payne."

Fuuuck!

Alex collapsed on the ground, using his equipment bag as a backrest as he pulled out his phone. He'd finally gotten Elijah out of his head for a couple hours, and the reporter had to go and bring him up again.

I'd really like to see you again. Call if you feel the same.

Those words were the first words bouncing around in his head each morning and the last words to settle when he went to bed at night. Usually after jacking off to what he and Elijah had done and what he would like to do.

It had taken some time, some soul searching, to conclude that he really wanted to see Elijah again.

Before Elijah had left the showers that day, the bastard had dropped that ticking emotional bomb in his lap, leaving it up to Alex to diffuse. But after ten days of no contact, what should he say? Was it too late?

He pulled up his messaging app, found Elijah's name, and started a text: *Hey.*

Lame.

He erased it and typed in: *What's up?*

Lamer. Sounded like a booty call.

Mashing the back button, he replaced the text with: *Wanna catch a beer?*

Better. But not what Alex really wanted.

The fourth time, the message read: *I would really like to see you some time. Give me a call.*

After hitting send, he added: *Or send me a text.*

He went to put his phone away, then added: *Or a fucking smoke signal.*

Jesus. He didn't know how to do this.

He stared down at his phone, willing the three little dots to show up, indicating Elijah was responding. He waited and waited some more. Then he started second guessing himself.

Someone clapped him on the arm, and he almost dropped his phone.

Trevor said, "Aren't you the eager one."

He dropped his phone into his bag. "I was... I was..."

Trevor took a step back. "Hey, man, why are you turning red?

I was talking about you being eager for the game. What did you think—"

Glancing from Alex to the phone he'd dropped in his bag, Trevor bent to pick it up.

Alex gave Trevor a playful shove away. "Get your glove and help warm me up. If I strain my elbow out here, I'm never going to let you hear the end of it."

In the next fifteen minutes, the rest of their team arrived as well as the competition. Alex's team captain, Greg, he thought his name was, assigned positions. His team had won the coin toss so they were the home team and would take the field first.

Greg threw Alex into right field, probably on Trevor's instruction. He started jogging out to right as Trevor jogged to first base.

"You suck," Alex teased. "I'm going to be so bored that I'm going to be picking daisies out there all night."

"You've got the best arm out here. If anyone can throw a guy out at home, it will be you. Besides, the long throws are good for your arm."

"Yeah, yeah," Alex grumbled as he jogged out to baseball Siberia.

The first guy at the plate struck out. The second and third got walked. Trevor glanced back at Alex, his hands out and shrugging his shoulders as if to say what-are-you-gonna-do-about-it.

Not that Alex could do anything about it. The rec league only agreed to let him play if he didn't pitch. Which wouldn't have been fair even if they'd allowed it. So, Alex stood there in right field, bored out of his ever-fucking-loving mind.

The next batter got a piece of the ball on a late, chopping, off-balance swing. The ball flew high in the air, in that no-man's land between first and right field. Alex tracked it as he ran forward. He had more speed and a better angle than the back-tracking Trevor.

"I got it, I got it," Alex hollered out, trying to call Trevor off the ball as it headed for foul territory by the visiting team's dugout. One of the guys from the visiting team said, "It's about time you got here."

As Alex camped out under the ball, he didn't pay the other player any attention, waiting to make the easy out. That's when Elijah said, "Sorry. Class ran late."

Alex turned, forgetting all about the ball. Hell, he forgot about the baseball game as Elijah walked up to the dugout with an equipment bag slung over his shoulder.

"What are you doing here?" Alex asked.

Stupid question.

The ball hit the chain link fence protecting the men in the dugout. Trevor ran over and picked it up, slapping Alex out of his stupor with backhanded glove to his ass. "Smooth, man. You ever thought of playing baseball professionally?"

———

ELIJAH'S TEAM LOST FIVE TO FOUR WHEN ALEX THREW ELIJAH OUT at home. Damn, that man had an arm. As Elijah packed up his gear, he turned down an invitation to go out to eat and grab a few beers with his teammates, mumbling lies about studying and tests and other general excuses.

He picked up miscellaneous trash left in the dugout, bubble gum wrappers, empty sunflower seed bags, half-drunk sports drink bottles, as he stalled, wanting to catch Alex alone before he left.

You have one hell of a masochistic streak. You told Alex to call if he was interested and there has been nothing but radio static ever since. Push him out of your head. Forget about him.

Move. The. Fuck. On.

That's what he'd do. Except he had to walk past Alex and some guy from Alex's team to get to his truck. Elijah shouldered his bag. Did he stop and say hello? Did he walk by with a nod of acknowledgment? Did he put his head down and keep on walking, pretending like they weren't even there?

You're over-thinking this.

But as he approached Alex and his friend, Alex broke his conversation and stepped toward Elijah. "Hey, you got a minute?"

"Uh... yeah, sure." He shouldn't get his hopes up, yet that didn't stop his heart from beating like it had when he'd rounded third base trying to beat Alex's throw from right field.

Breathe, Elijah.

The other man came over as well and said, "Hey, man, aren't you—"

Alex stripped the equipment bag off his friend's shoulder and tossed it toward the parking lot. "Beat it, dickhead."

The guy laughed and stuck out his hand. "Trevor Moon. Don't mind my friend. He has no manners."

Elijah shook his hand, "I'm—"

"Elijah," Trevor said with a wink. *Did people still wink?* "Yeah, trust me, I know."

Alex took Trevor by the shoulders and physically turned him toward the parking lot and gave him a playful shove. "Go. I'll see you in the morning."

"Fine. I know when I'm not wanted." Trevor picked up his bag again and slung it over his shoulder. "Come ready to kick ass tomorrow, Payne. I've got a new exercise for your arm that I think we should try." Then to Elijah, "Nice to finally meet you."

"You, too."

"So?" That one little word from Alex's mouth dipped low

and intimate, making Elijah hard. At least the athletic cup would hide his arousal.

Alex shoved his hands into his back pockets and rocked back on his heels. The expectant expression on Alex's face made Elijah feel like he'd been daydreaming when his professor asked him a question. What had he missed?

"Sooo?" Elijah repeated when what he wanted to ask was why Alex had never called or texted.

The fact was, Alex *hadn't*. Which *was* an answer.

When the silence dragged, Elijah added, "Look, this doesn't have to be awkward. We don't have to acknowledge each other on the field when our teams play each other if that's what you want."

A slow smile spread on Alex's face. Elijah was missing something. "Is that what you want?"

"No." Was that too quick? Too eager? Shit. He didn't want to scare Alex away. "You?"

Alex shook his head, that damn smile taking over his face. "I take it you didn't get my text."

"I was running late. Forgot my phone at the apartment." Then it really hit Elijah what Alex had said, what it *meant*. "You texted."

"I did. Which means I do. I mean, not *I do*, I do, but 'I do' in that I would like to see you again. So maybe check your schedule and, I don't know, we can meet up somewhere... for something."

"Somewhere for something?" Elijah chuckled and hitched the strap of his equipment bag higher on his shoulder to stop it from slipping. "You're adorable when you're flustered. You know that?"

"Jesus Christ." Alex huffed out a laugh and adjusted his baseball cap as he stared off toward the parking lot. "That was pretty lame, wasn't it?"

"I take it you don't date much?"

Alex blew out a long breath, then looked up at Elijah under the brim of his baseball cap. "Not men. Or any man. I mean... I'm fucking this up."

Holy crap. Alex is asking you out! Say yes, you idiot. "You're not. And I'm free."

"What?" Alex visibly relaxed.

"Now. I'm free now. To do *something, somewhere.*"

And honestly, he didn't care that he sounded too eager. Alex obviously had some things he'd had to sort in his head before deciding to ask Elijah out. He wasn't going to wait another ten days and give Alex the chance to change his mind.

The field lights went out, pitching them into near darkness, only the security lights spilling out from the parking lot provided illumination.

"I guess that's our cue," Alex said as they started walking back to their vehicles. "Now's good. What do you want to do?"

Fuck you was the first thing that jumped to mind, but that was Elijah's amped-up libido talking. Since the last time he'd seen Alex, he'd had plenty of time to think about what it would mean if Alex called. All the scientists would have to recalibrate their charts to be able to log his and Alex's sexual chemistry, but in the waiting, Elijah had come to realize he wanted a lot more from Alex than random, no-strings-attached sex.

"We could go grab a couple beers."

In the dull light, Alex's face scrunched up. "You probably don't want to be seen with me in public and have to dodge reporters. I'd rather spend some time alone with you."

Elijah wouldn't want to be seen with Alex? Or Alex didn't want to be seen with him?

"Then what do you want to do?" At the parking lot, Elijah tossed his equipment bag into the back of his truck.

"I could help you with your swing."

"That bad?"

One of Alex's shoulders bobbed up and down. One of those yeah-but-I'm-not-gonna-come-right-out-and-say-it shrugs. "I know a place where we won't be bothered."

"Lead the way."

Alex plopped his bag in the back of Elijah's truck. "Let's leave my car here for now. It's not exactly inconspicuous."

"The reporters still giving you problems?" Elijah unlocked his truck and Alex went around, and they both climbed in.

"It's gotten a lot better, but they pop up in unlikely places. I think..." Alex buckled his seatbelt and stared out the windshield as if trying to choose his words carefully. "I think that it would be best if people don't see us together right now is all."

On some level, Elijah had expected this, but to hear it come out of Alex's mouth... Elijah's stomach knotted into a tight ball ten times harder than a baseball.

Elijah needed a life he could live as himself with integrity. He couldn't live a life of deceit.

Not anymore.

Elijah buckled his seatbelt, more for the emotional ride he was about to take than the physical. "Before this goes anywhere, to be clear, I'm not going to be anyone's dirty little secret."

"That's not—"

"Let me finish."

When Alex nodded, Elijah continued. "I get it. You have more at stake with your career right now than I do. So, I'm good with keeping us on the downlow. For now. But I'm not going to live my life in the closet ashamed of who I am and who I'm attracted to. For you. Or for anybody. I lived that life for too many years in the military. If you need to take some time and think about it and get back to me. I'm okay with that."

Alex leaned across the center console and pressed a kiss to Elijah's lips, but didn't take it any further. Elijah almost reached for Alex as he settled into his seat, wanting to buzz his seat back and pull Alex across the console. The physical impossibility of it was the only thing stopping him.

Elijah started the engine.

"This is just for right now," Alex insisted. "A few weeks. A month maybe. At least until we get to know each other a little better. Who knows, after I give you a batting lesson, you may never want to see me again."

———

Alex gave Elijah directions to SFSC. When they parked out of view behind the sports complex, they were the only vehicle in the lot.

Elijah kept the engine running. "We're too late. This place looks closed."

Alex unbuckled and popped the latch on the door. "Not for us."

Elijah killed the engine, beeped the truck locked and met him at the tailgate. "Well, aren't *you* special?"

A self-deprecating laugh escaped. There had been a time when Alex had thought that he *was* special, but the game of fate had a way of knocking him down peg by peg by peg without mercy until he'd been left dangling by his fingertips.

He had talent.

He had perseverance.

But that didn't make him special.

"Hardly. I've known the owner since his kid and I played little league together. He's kind enough to let me have a key."

Alex unlocked the door and disarmed the alarm, ushering Elijah inside ahead of him so he could lock the door behind them. The sparse security lights provided illumination down the long back hall. They'd both changed out of their spikes at the field, so only the soft squeak and scuff of their athletic shoes echoed off the hard surfaces.

After hours at the complex was one of Alex's favorite places to go when he wanted to be alone and have time to think. The Grizzlies were a part of the American League, so as a pitcher he didn't have to hit, but that didn't mean he didn't like to pick up a bat from time to time and take some hacks in the cages until his hands stung and his muscles screamed with fatigue.

At the long row of batting cages, Alex dropped his bag and turned on the banks of overhead lights. He took Elijah and their bats into the center cage as the lights slowly warmed up.

"You want to go first?" Alex asked.

"You get it out of your system, then we'll worry about me."

Alex hit for several rounds before turning the cage over to Elijah, enjoying the lingering sting in his hands and the burn in his shoulders.

"First thing I noticed," Alex said, "is that you're very long to the ball. It makes it harder for you to catch up to the faster pitches and makes it nearly impossible to hit anything up and in. And your swing isn't level, so you're getting underneath the ball. That's why you're getting the pop-ups."

"Was I doing anything right?" Elijah crossed his arms, the three-quarter sleeves of his uniform bulging at his biceps.

Alex wanted to drop the bat, strip off Elijah's shirt and get another feel for those muscles himself. But they had all night for that. He grinned. "You knew where to stand in the batter's box, so you weren't a complete embarrassment to the sport."

"Fucker," Elijah muttered, but he couldn't hide his smile.

That's one of the things he liked about Elijah, he wasn't an insecure man, even when faced with something he wasn't particularly skilled at. After being on Black Stallion's set with the man, Alex knew Elijah to be particularly knowledgeable, confident, and competent in other areas of his life.

Alex took several practice swings. Demonstrating how Elijah had been swinging versus how he should be bringing the bat to the ball. Then it was Elijah's turn, and Alex stepped back.

"Hands a little higher. Yeah, like that. Now start your swing by bringing the knob toward the ball."

After a few slo-mo swings, Alex said, "Hang on, I'll be right back."

He hustled out of the cage and retrieved Elijah's batting helmet. After Elijah put it on, Alex said, "Ready?"

"Bring it on."

Alex flipped the switch, and the pitching machine at the other end of the cage came to life: humming, clacking, and wheezing. Then he turned down the speed, pressed start, and stepped out of the cage. "Let the first couple pitches go by so you can judge how the balls are coming out of the machine."

Two pitches zinged by Elijah as he stood ready in the batter's box, the balls hitting the hanging mat at the back of the cage with a loud thud. Elijah touched the far side of the plate with the tip of his bat and got ready for the next pitch, his muscular ass shaking as he dug into position.

By the time Elijah had hit his way through two and a half rounds of balls, he'd started hitting better, but his swing was off, and no matter how much Alex tried to correct him from outside the cage, he couldn't get his point across.

Some things needed more personal instruction.

Alex entered the cage and hit the pause button. Elijah dropped the end of his bat and turned. "What's wrong?"

Bumping his chin toward the batter's box, Alex said, "I'm going to help you with your swing. Stand in the batter's box, and I'll show you."

Elijah got his feet set and brought the bat back. Alex came up behind him and put his hands on Elijah's hips. Elijah dropped the head of the bat. "What are you doing?"

"I'm not getting fresh."

"Shame."

Alex gave Elijah's hips a little squeeze. "Don't get me started. We're hitting. Not... not anything else."

Yeah, tell that to the woody you're sporting.

Elijah lifted the bat as Alex said, "Your power is in your hips, you don't want to open them too soon or else you'll lose all your power before you can turn on the ball."

Elijah swung several times in slow motion with Alex turning his hips at the proper time in the swing. Unfortunately, that meant a lot of Alex's focus was on that firm, round, muscular ass. All Alex wanted to do was rut up against Elijah.

But he was a grown man. He had more control than that.

Ha! Yeah. Nice one.

Confident Elijah had the idea of how to move his hips, Alex said, "Now for your swing."

Alex let go of Elijah's hips, stepping closer so that his arms came around Elijah's shoulders, his hands on the bat on top of Elijah's hands. Elijah wiggled his ass, and Alex swallowed a groan. Was Elijah settling into his stance or was he trying to press his ass into Alex's crotch? Elijah did it again. "You're gonna have to quit that," Alex said, but didn't move away.

Elijah chuckled. "I'm standing here minding my own business. You're the one who put his arms around me."

Elijah wasn't wrong, so Alex didn't argue. They worked through the swing together, their bodies aligned from shoulders to hips to thighs. Since Alex had taken his athletic cup out in the dugout, there were only a few layers of fabric between them, and those layers did a piss poor job of hiding his erection.

Not that Elijah complained.

Then Alex moved to leave the cage and give Elijah room to swing, but instead of getting ready in the batter's box, Elijah dropped his bat on the ground. It rolled until the side wall of the cage stopped it.

"What's the matter?"

Elijah pulled his batting gloves off his fingers one by one as he closed the gap between them. He backed Alex up against the gate, the chain link pressing little diamond shapes into the muscles in his back.

"I've already taken a lot of cuts. I'm afraid if I keep batting, I'm going to lose my grip strength."

Linking his fingers in the fencing by Alex's head, Elijah leaned in, his breath warm on Alex's skin as he pressed kisses to Alex's neck and the corner of his jaw. Elijah's other hand trailed down the length of Alex's torso and down farther until he cupped Alex's hard cock in his hand.

"*Gnnpff.*" Alex pressed into Elijah's hand, craving the contact.

With a hand to the back of Elijah's neck, Alex brought Elijah's lips to his. Elijah opened his mouth, and his tongue darted out, tracing Alex's lower lip. Alex opened for him with a groan as Elijah stroked him through his uniform pants.

Alex broke the kiss. "We gotta stop."

Elijah's eyes closed but he lifted his hands and took a step back. "I'm sorry if I misread this. I thought—"

"Shit. No. You didn't misinterpret anything." Alex scrubbed a hand down his face. "I didn't mean 'stop' that way. I meant we need to stop so we can go somewhere that isn't here. Somewhere that doesn't have security cameras. Somewhere that we can take our time and not have to worry about someone walking in on us and for once not have to hear someone yelling 'cut.'"

Elijah blinked at him a couple times, then a smile started at the corners of his mouth. "You want to go to your place?"

"Yours is closer if you live near the college campus."

"I do."

"I don't want anyone seeing my car there. You drive. You

could take me back to mine..." The next words out of Alex's mouth would be presumptuous, but he wanted to be direct. "...in the morning."

Alex held his breath. Did he really invite himself over to spend the night? He did, didn't he? Was that rude?

"My place it is."

They gathered the gear, high-tailed it to the parking lot, and headed to Elijah's apartment. In the tree-lined parking lot near the soccer fields, across the street from the complex, the lights on a parked car turned on. Alex watched in his side mirror as the car pulled out onto the road behind him.

"What is it?" Elijah asked, his wrist dangling over the top of the steering wheel, the hint of a laugh in his voice. "We pick up a tail?"

Trevor always talked about how the closet makes a man paranoid.

Alex turned and watched out the rear window as the car faded back and two other vehicles passed and pulled in between them. He turned back around, shoving the car out of his mind.

Alex wasn't paranoid.

He also wasn't in the closet.

Oh yeah? How many straight guys go home with their male porn co-stars to fuck around?

11

———

THAT SAYING 'GIDDY AS A SCHOOLGIRL' RAN THROUGH ELIJAH'S mind. His hand shook, and he fumbled with his keys as he tried to unlock his apartment door. Only Elijah wasn't a schoolgirl, he was a grown ass man.

A grown ass man taking another man to his apartment for sex.

He wasn't a virgin by far, but Alex was the only man he'd had any sexual contact with, and well... that made him a little nervous. What if they started having sex and Alex didn't like it?

What if *he* didn't like it?

Kissing and mutual blow jobs were one thing, going beyond was another. But God help him, he was ready to try.

Alex put a hand over Elijah's and steadied it long enough for him to get the key in the lock and shove the door open. Elijah flipped lights on as he walked down the hall to his kitchen and den.

He went straight for the refrigerator and tugged it open. "You want a beer?"

Alex stood in the den and glanced around. "That would be great. Thanks."

Elijah grabbed the beers and met Alex at the patio door where Alex stared through the open slats of the vertical blinds. Elijah flipped a switch. The porch lights lit up the patio of his first-floor apartment, the trees in the park behind his unit nearly overhanging his fence.

His apartment wasn't much to look at, and the maintenance department was run by a man who didn't know a slotted screwdriver from a Phillips head, but having the trees to look at instead of a parking lot or the bedroom of another apartment made what little extra he paid for the place worth it.

Elijah handed Alex a beer and worked the stubborn mechanism of the blinds as he tried to slide them back. Then something above snapped, and the cord came loose in his hands. "Shit. I wanted to show you the view." Elijah flipped the lock on the sliding door. "We can—"

Alex put a staying hand on Elijah's arm, his gaze scorching. "It's okay. I like the view in here better."

Elijah took a fortifying sip of his beer. "You hungry?"

Alex backed Elijah into the sliding door and set both of their beers onto a shelf on the nearby entertainment center. The blue around Alex's irises going thin as his pupils dilated. "Yeah." Alex nipped at Elijah's chin. "But not for food."

Alex stepped a leg between Elijah's and pressed his erection against Elijah's hip. With the cold glass at Elijah's back, déjà vu washed over him, only this time the view out the window was of a six-foot privacy fence and not a fake New York City skyline.

In other ways, this experience was completely different. They didn't have to worry about camera angles, about people on set, and about Niko calling out directions.

The biggest difference?... They had all night.

Alex untucked Elijah's uniform shirt and yanked it over his head. Alex's hand immediately went to Elijah's thick slab of pectoral muscle, his thumb skimming across Elijah's flat nipple.

Horny Elijah kicked Nervous Elijah to the curb. Time to get what he wanted.

"Get naked," Elijah said, part growl and part command as his fingers fumbled with Alex's belt.

In a flurry of feverish activity, they both toed off their shoes, and shucked their uniforms and sliding shorts. They were both short of breath, more from anticipation than exertion when they stood straight.

"Damn," Alex said, his voice gruff as he took in Elijah from his toes to his jutting cock and on up to his face.

Alex linked fingers with Elijah, pinning Elijah's hands against the glass above his head, their bodies aligned, their hard-ons trapped together between their bellies. "You're so *fucking* sexy."

Alex may have had Elijah beat on height, but Elijah had Alex beat on sheer muscle mass, and there was nothing Elijah enjoyed more than control. He turned, reversing their positions, their feet tangling. Alex's back hit the open blinds and sliding glass door with a thunk, and their combined off-balance weight took them to the ground.

They hit in a pile of legs, arms, torsos, and cocks, Alex laughing as three of the slats from the blinds tumbled down on top of them.

Elijah batted the cheap plastic away. The building's maintenance guy was going to be pissed, but Elijah couldn't give two shits right then, not when Alex lay beneath him, their cocks leaking pre-cum on the flat of Alex's lower abs.

Bracing himself on one arm, Elijah brought his mouth to Alex's as his other hand wrapped around their erections and he started jacking them both.

Alex grumbled into Elijah's mouth. Something like, "Oh God."

His arms slid down Elijah's back, those long fingers reaching down and squeezing Elijah's ass. A lone index finger rode along Elijah's crack as Alex rutted up against him.

Pre-cum slicked Elijah's hand as he stroked them from tip to base and back again. He buried his face in the crook of Alex's neck, inhaling the intoxicating smell of musky sweat, aged leather, and diamond dirt, finding it much more arousing than the clean scent of soap.

Alex cupped Elijah's cheek bringing Elijah's mouth up to his and taking the kiss deep. Alex's tongue thrust into Elijah's mouth, mimicking what Elijah wanted Alex to do to his ass.

Alex's tongue wasn't the only thing Elijah wanted in his ass, he wanted Alex's fingers and that glorious cock.

What if Alex doesn't want to go there? What if kissing, mutual masturbation, and blow jobs were all that Alex wanted?

Breaking the kiss, Elijah took a couple moments to catch his breath.

"I do something wrong?" Alex's finger hesitated in the crack of Elijah's ass.

"No. I wanted to ask what you were into."

Alex's brows drew together as if Elijah had asked a confusing question. Elijah rolled onto his back, shifting Alex to his side. Alex drew a hand down the length of Elijah's body until he had Elijah's balls cupped in his hands. Elijah's eyes tried to cross as goosebumps skittered across his flesh.

"I thought I was making myself clear." Alex pressed a series of kisses across Elijah's chest, his tongue flicking across Elijah's sensitized nipple, sending a zing straight through to Elijah's dick. "I'm into you."

It pained Elijah to stop the magic Alex made with his tongue, but things weren't as cut and dried in gay sex land as it was in hetero sex land. A little more negotiation was involved. Not everyone was into ass or getting fucked.

Elijah put a staying hand on Alex's chest, and Alex removed

his hand from between Elijah's thighs. "I mean what are you into, as in, what do you like to do or have done to you?"

Alex propped his head on his hand, looking down on Elijah as he ghosted his fingertips through the short, cropped hair around Elijah's base. He wanted to take Alex's hand and fist it around his cock and forget all about talking, but this wasn't a conversation they could put off.

Alex didn't answer right away, though Elijah could hear the gears in Alex's head click and churn. Finally, Alex said, "I like head. Receiving and giving. I want your hands on me and mine on you and…"

Elijah could tell Alex had more to say, he just needed the time to figure out the words to say it. Elijah waited him out, not wanting to push or put words in Alex's mouth.

Alex took a deep breath then blew it out. "I don't know if I'm ready to be fucked… It's not that I'm necessarily against it… It's…"

Alex sort of squirmed, and realization dawned on Elijah. "You've never done any ass play."

"I have. The giving end, not the receiving end."

Elijah grinned. "You don't know what you're missing."

Alex chuckled and rolled his eyes. "That's what Trevor keeps telling me." Then those eyes narrowed and focused on Elijah. "Wait, you told Niko you've never been with a guy before."

"I haven't."

"Then how…?"

"I had this kinky girlfriend who loved to peg me with a strap on." All that talk about anal sex, clinical as it was, turned Elijah the fuck on. Reaching down, he started stroking himself.

Alex's eyes followed Elijah's hand for a stroke or two then brought his focus up to Elijah's face. "How was it?"

"Hot as hell."

"*Jesus Christ.*" Alex's eyes went dark, his nostrils flared, and he went in for another kiss, his tongue tasting, devouring.

Alex broke the kiss long enough for them to catch their breath. Elijah's heart kicked at his sternum, full, high kicks—an audition for *A Chorus Line*, as the flood of blood whooshed past his eardrums.

Elijah could see the need for more in Alex's eyes, feel it in the way Alex's hand kneaded the flesh at Elijah's hip. Alex just required a nudge and Elijah was certain Alex would jump in head first. "Tell me what you want."

Alex swallowed hard, his eyes locking on Elijah's when he said, "I want your ass."

———

ALEX STOOD AT THE SLIDING DOOR, GLANCING UP AT THE TREES illuminated by Elijah's porch light while he waited for Elijah to return. He thought he'd seen movement, but the wind had picked up, and the branches were swaying and—

"What the f—" Alex jumped back from the sliding door, as adrenaline dumped into his already ramped up system.

"What's wrong?" Elijah called out from his bedroom.

A fucking cat. Alex's hand went to his chest as if that could slow his racing heart. "A black cat jumped onto the patio from the tree. I didn't know you had a cat."

Elijah returned with lube and condoms. While they had both been tested twice through Black Stallion, the time between testing had been narrow so they'd opted to be cautious and go with condoms.

"Neighbor's cat. He likes my patio chairs."

As if proving the point, the cat jumped up on one of the chairs, curled up, and closed its golden eyes. Alex's heart settled, and after one last look around, he shut off the patio light and turned toward Elijah.

Elijah set the lube on the scratched and dented wood coffee table and handed him the condom.

"You sure you're good with this?" Alex asked, trying not to sound too eager when all he wanted was to get his hands on that tight, round ass.

Elijah took the condom back, ripped the packet open with his teeth and slipped it over the tip of Alex's dick. Elijah's eyes narrowed, but there was no anger behind it. "You're not scroting out on me are you, number twenty-three?"

The only time Alex had worn that number was on his one and only day in the majors. Alex grinned. "You've done your homework."

Excruciatingly slowly, Elijah rolled the condom down. "I've always been the studious type."

"Teacher's pet, I'll bet." Alex backed Elijah up until Elijah's thighs hit the rolled armrest of the black leather couch and he had nowhere else to go.

"Except when I'm naughty."

Alex placed a hand on Elijah's hip, encouraging him to turn around. "Bend over." His words came out gruff, strangled—part need, part nerves.

He wasn't so much nervous about where he wanted to put his dick. It was more than that. To Alex, this wasn't a casual hookup, which made the stakes so much higher. For the first time in a long time, he really cared that he was good, that he would please Elijah. Despite all of Alex's questions about his sexuality, about himself, he knew for sure that he wanted to see Elijah again.

Elijah gave him one last searing kiss, one that made his heart light, his balls heavy, and his balls tight, then bent over the armrest of the couch. Alex stepped up behind him, lodging the length of himself in the crack of Elijah's ass. He ran his hands down Elijah's torso, from those broad shoulders, past the cut ribs and narrow waist to the two most perfect ass cheeks he'd ever laid eyes on. And, considering Alex's profession, he considered himself well versed in naked male ass.

Alex skimmed a reverent hand over the muscled curve of Elijah's cheek. "*Fuuck*... that ass—"

Alex didn't get a chance to finish his sentence before Elijah glanced at him over his shoulder, a smile on his face and devilment in his eyes. "That's what I'm trying to tell you."

Alex chuckled, giving one globe a light smack as he sunk to his knees. The cheap tile was hard on his knees, but he hardly noticed as he sat back on his legs and parted Elijah's cheeks. He nipped at the thick muscle, leaving tiny teeth marks that drew a grunt of approval out of Elijah.

Then Alex dove in, drawing his tongue up Elijah's taint to the star of muscle. Elijah hissed in a breath, the leather of the couch squeaking beneath Elijah's grip. Alex stayed there for a time, licking and tasting, his own cock granite hard as Elijah ground his ass against Alex's face.

Then he stood, and reached for the lube, spreading some on his fingers and a healthy dose on his aching cock. Elijah glanced over, his face flushed, his eyes hooded and needy. "Hurry the hell up."

Alex groaned, leaning over and pressing a kiss along Elijah's spine. Goosebumps erupted, pebbling Elijah's skin. "I like you when you're grumpy, bossy, and horny."

Gripping Elijah's hip, Alex lubed up Elijah's hole, the muscle tightening at his touch. Slowly, Alex worked one finger in and out, Elijah moving with and against the pressure, and Elijah collapsed over the armrest and rested his forehead on the cushion between his forearms.

Alex eased in a second finger and eventually a third, the tight muscle contracting then giving as Elijah breathed and relaxed. *Jesus, that was sexy.* "You were quick to take my fingers."

Elijah thrust back, fucking himself on Alex's digits. "After my girlfriend, I became a big fan of dildos and butt plugs when I jack off."

Alex's cock jerked. If Elijah kept talking like that, Alex was going to cum before he'd had a chance to put his dick in.

Leaning over, Alex nipped and kissed Elijah's shoulder. Alex scissored his fingers and Elijah sucked in a deep breath and let it out on a low groan that had pre-cum filling the tip of Alex's condom.

He wanted—needed—to bury himself between those cheeks.

"You ready?" Alex asked.

Elijah rose, bracing his hands on the seat cushion. "Shut up and fuck me already."

Alex wasn't one to keep an impatient man waiting, especially one with as fine an ass as Elijah had. And to be honest, Alex couldn't wait any longer himself.

He parted Elijah's cheeks, those glorious globes flexing and contracting in Alex's hands. Then he laid the head of his cock at Elijah's hole and pressed in.

"*Holy hell,*" Elijah breathed out, his head dropping between his arms, a thin layer of sweat breaking out across his skin.

"Want me to stop?"

"Don't you dare."

Alex pulled out a fraction, then started a shallow thrust. Damn Elijah was tight. Inch by inch, Alex watched as Elijah's greedy hole swallowed him down until he was balls deep.

No woman had ever been able to take all of him. Having that tight squeeze at his base had Alex's balls drawing up tight and the tingle starting at the base of his spine.

Alex clenched his jaw and stilled. He wasn't going to last.

Before he could start sliding out, Elijah said, "Give me a minute."

Elijah blew out a couple of deep breaths, the grip on his dick loosened a fraction. Alex ran his hands up and down Elijah's sides, across the expanse of shoulder blades, then let his fingers bump down Elijah's backbone, past the line where his tan gave way to pale skin.

"Go," Elijah said. "Slow."

Alex pulled most of the way out, reached for the lube and added more to be on the safe side. Then it was another long, slow dive back in.

Elijah reached a hand back to Alex's hip, encouraging him to move faster, harder. Each thrust ended with a grunt from Alex and a groan from Elijah, Alex's balls slapping against Elijah's. As their rhythm picked up, Elijah reached down and took himself in his hand, his stroke speed mimicking Alex's thrusts.

"Harder," Elijah said, as his grunts grew thicker, his pants more breathless.

Alex drove harder, the sensations building, as his lungs billowed and his heart tripped and stumbled, trying like hell to keep up.

"Harder, scrote."

Alex barked a laugh, upping his tempo, the couch scooting with each powerful thrust. Then the sensations, the grip, the slide, the sounds, the scents, were too much, and Alex had no hope of holding out any longer.

His thrusts went erratic, and the first pulses of his release hit. "I'm coming." The words came out on the heels of harsh pants.

Elijah jacked off faster, which only made Alex come harder. Alex stiffened above Elijah, his hands gripping Elijah's hips as he held Elijah's deliciously sweaty ass tight against him as he came and came.

With his lungs burning, his quads screaming, Alex slumped against Elijah, arms hugging Elijah to his chest as Elijah went still. "*Fuuuck.*"

As Elijah came, his ass tightened rhythmically around Alex's cock, milking the last drops, and a sated moan came out of him. Alex released Elijah, and straightened, not wanting to pull out even as he started to go soft. He ran his hands all over Elijah's body, enjoying the feel of the tight ball of muscle capping Elijah's shoulder and the way Elijah's arms quivered and his legs shook from exertion and pleasure.

Slowly, Alex pulled out and gave Elijah a hand up. Sweat beaded on Elijah's forehead and dripped down the valley between his pecs. Elijah put his arms around Alex's neck, and they clung together as their breathing and heart rate returned to normal. "That was..." Elijah started.

"Fucking amazing."

Elijah kissed his way across Alex's collarbone and up his neck to the corner of Alex's jaw. In his ear, Elijah said, "I love your cock."

———

ELIJAH WOKE TO A WARM BODY CURLED AROUND HIS, ALEX'S ARM draped across his hip, and Alex's morning wood snuggled nicely into the crack of Elijah's ass. Elijah could get used to waking up like this, his own balls heavy and his hard-on aching for release.

Rolling onto his back, Elijah found Alex already awake, staring down at him. "Morning."

"Actually," Alex said, "it's almost noon."

"Noon?" Elijah bolted upright. He had class and—

Alex pushed him back into the pillow. "You've already missed your class, and I've missed my PT." Then Alex leaned in, nuzzled the sensitive skin along Elijah's neck. "Might as well stay in bed and enjoy what's left of the day."

Elijah laughed, but it came out tight and rueful.

"What's so funny?" Alex shifted, throwing a leg over Elijah's as he ran his hands across Elijah's lower abdomen.

"A part of me thought I'd wake up and you'd be gone. That what we'd shared and done last night would have freaked you the fuck out. I hadn't anticipated waking up with you in my bed, wanting to do it all over again."

"I don't have a car," Alex deadpanned, but he couldn't hold a straight face for long. "Even if my car were here, I hadn't planned on going anywhere until I had to."

"Why?"

Alex's hand stalled on Elijah's abdomen, and the smile slipped from his face. "Because I like being with you. Because I enjoy touching you and kissing you and fucking you."

Alex nipped on Elijah's earlobe and caressed Elijah's hip, and all Elijah wanted to do was sink into their mutual pleasure. In Elijah's ear, Alex said, "I want to stick around and see where this can go. And I'm not just talking about the sex."

Elijah wanted to believe him, he really did, but he wasn't convinced Alex had thought through what a relationship with him would mean, personally, socially, professionally.

As quickly as Elijah was developing feelings for Alex, if Alex jumped, Elijah wanted him to do it equipped with a parachute, safety gear, and both eyes wide open. He didn't want to be the one held responsible if Alex fell and went splat.

"I'm not hiding who I am. I'm not going back into the closet for you or anybody."

"I'm not asking you to do that." Alex slid his hand down, reaching for Elijah's cock.

Elijah placed a staying hand on Alex's and eased away. If Elijah allowed Alex to put his hands on him, they both knew the talking would be over. But this was serious. It wasn't something they could gloss over.

"But you have, implicitly if not outright. The whole taking

my truck and going to my place instead of yours. You wouldn't have to do that if you weren't trying to hide me or us."

Alex rolled off his side of the bed and stood. The ticking of the blood vessel at Alex's temple and the hard line of Alex's mouth told Elijah he'd struck a nerve.

"I'm not. It's... With my career, it's... complicated."

"Tell me about it." Elijah climbed out of bed and headed for the toilet. He had no trouble peeing because his morning wood had evaporated.

When he flushed and turned around, Alex stood behind him in all his naked glory, his arms spanning the doorway. Elijah could have muscled his way through, but for some reason, he didn't.

"It's nobody's business who I sleep with," Alex said, "but that doesn't keep people from trying to make it their business. In this day and age, it shouldn't be an issue to be out and playing ball professionally, but it is. Statistically speaking, there must be scores of closeted players in the sport. But I get it. When being out can ruin your career, everything you've worked so hard for... I get it. Even if it doesn't make it right."

Elijah stuck out his chin, almost daring Alex. "Someone's got to be the first."

Alex's gaze dropped, then came back up, his expression almost apologetic. After blowing out a breath, he said, "Honestly? I don't know if I'm that guy."

A tightness constricted Elijah's chest. Alex's words shouldn't have hurt as much as they did.

You're falling for him.

Elijah wanted to laugh but couldn't find the humor.

As much as Elijah wanted a chance to see where a relationship with Alex would go, those words... those words told him a relationship couldn't, and wouldn't, go anywhere.

Elijah cleared his throat. "Fair enough."

He brushed past Alex as a knock came at his door. Elijah reached for a towel and wrapped it around his waist. "You should get dressed. I'll take you to your car."

Alex stopped him with a hand on his shoulder. The knock came again, more insistent as Alex came up behind Elijah and wrapped his arms around Elijah's shoulders from behind, the pounding of Alex's heart thrummed against his spine.

Alex ducked his head and said, "I'm asking for a little time to sort this out. Can you give that to me?"

Elijah didn't respond. Giving Alex more time. More time to worm his way under Elijah's skin and into his heart and his life was a bad, bad idea. Better to cut Alex loose now and avoid the hurt than risk the inescapable devastation later.

Too late. That tightness in your throat. That stinging in your chest. That heavy way your stomach is sitting in your abdomen. That's pain.

And when Alex said, "Please," in Elijah's ear, with that rough and raw emotion, and the tender kiss pressed against Elijah's warm flesh, Elijah knew the pain, the hurt, was only beginning.

Elijah swallowed hard, knowing he was about to make the biggest mistake of his life. "Okay."

With a peck to Elijah's neck, Alex said, "You won't regret this."

The pounding made Elijah's front door shudder in its frame. If Elijah didn't know any better, he'd think S.W.A.T was at his door with a battering ram.

"Elijah!" came Demetri's voice through the door. "Open the damn door."

Alex followed Elijah out of the bedroom and headed for the clothes they'd discarded in a pile by the sliding glass door.

"I'm coming, I'm coming." Elijah threw the locks on the door and opened it a crack.

Demetri barged through, a curt, "Lock the door," falling from his lips.

"Why aren't you answering your phone?" Demetri said as he stormed down the hallway. He came up short by the kitchen at the sight of a naked Alex slipping into his sliding shorts. "Well, that explains it."

"Explains what?" Alex picked up his pants and turned them right side out.

"You might want to get away from the glass door," Demetri said as he disappeared into the bedroom.

"What's going on?"

Elijah could only shrug. Demetri returned from the bedroom with Elijah's comforter and draped it over the top of the blinds, cutting out the natural light.

Elijah flipped a switch for the overhead light. "What the hell is going on? Why are you here?"

The polite side of Demetri had him reaching across the coffee table and introducing himself to Alex.

Elijah put his hands on his hips. This wasn't a time for niceties. "*Demetri?*"

Demetri made a face as if it pained him to have to say what he'd come to say. "Niko wants to talk to the both of you. He's been trying to get hold of you guys ever since the video dropped."

12

———————

"W—what video?"

Alex almost couldn't spit the words out as he finished getting dressed. Something whirred in his ears. Blood? Or the sound of what was left of his career swirling down the toilet?

Not only had he fucked Elijah, but in doing so had he done something to completely fuck his career as well?

Elijah grabbed his laptop off the end table and opened it on the kitchen bar. Alex and Demetri gathered around. When the computer booted up, Elijah turned it toward Demetri who typed in the website for one of the nationally syndicated tabloids.

Alex wrapped his arms around his head, almost afraid to look, but more afraid not to.

Maybe he and Elijah had been filmed coming and going from the sports complex. He'd been so psyched and turned on by the idea of finally getting with Elijah that they might have kissed and held hands and generally been all over each other as they'd stumbled to Elijah's truck in their rush to get back to the apartment. Which definitely would have been more difficult to explain away than doing gay porn for cash.

Being caught kissing and holding hands outside of Black

Stallion would have been bad enough, like a lit firecracker in your hand. You know it's going to suck when it goes off, but it would be survivable.

Trevor clicked on the link in the story and the video that played on the screen was like being duct taped to the reactor at Chernobyl—shit was about to get real.

The video on screen had been shot through the open and broken slats of Elijah's sliding glass door. With those three slats missing, there wasn't much left to the imagination as Alex plowed into Elijah from behind.

"I'm so fucked," Alex said.

"Actually," Demetri closed the lid on the laptop, "from the looks of it, it was Elijah who—"

Elijah elbowed Demetri in the gut. "Not funny."

"Why are you here again?" Alex couldn't drum up enough spit to swallow. He reached into Elijah's fridge for a bottle of water. Maybe his brain was dehydrated from all the sex, and that was why he couldn't think straight.

Straight. There was that word. Mocking him.

"Niko sent me. He wants to see you at the studios. Now."

Elijah leaned a toweled hip against the bar, his arms folded across his chest. There was no question why Niko wanted to see them. "Can't he fire us over the phone?"

"He's shooting today. Besides, he says he wants to see you two in person. ASAP." Demetri raised his hands and started backing out of the room. "I'm just the messenger."

Elijah and Alex followed him to the door. Demetri had his hand on the knob, his demeanor softening when he turned. "This shit's going to blow over. Don't let it destroy what you two have."

Have? Did they have anything besides the ability to make each other come every time they got together?

A part of Alex had dared to hope. But that was before.

Alex huffed out a laugh, but could the sound really be called a laugh when he couldn't see the humor in any of this? "Too late."

Elijah's face fell, and he had one of those surprised and betrayed looks on his face, the kind actors get on screen when someone they trusted thrusts a knife into their chest. Alex wanted to take his words back, but he couldn't take back the truth.

"How bad is it out there?" Alex asked. Maybe they could get to Black Stallion, get their meeting with Niko over with, and then he could steal a few hours to figure out how to dig himself out of the crater that was left of his career.

Demetri winced. "The group out there makes your last round of press attention look like amateur hour."

Demetri left, and Alex and Elijah wasted no time showering and dressing. No way was Alex going through the day smelling Elijah all over him. It would be like holding a bone in front of the starving dog. He didn't need that constant reminder of what he shouldn't, or couldn't, allow himself to have.

At least not right now.

Not until he'd repaired his career.

If that were even possible.

An ESPN news truck pulled into the apartment parking lot as Alex and Elijah fought their way through the press to Elijah's truck. The morning-after walk of shame was bad enough when there weren't twenty cameras and fists full of microphones being shoved in your face.

"Alex, Alex," one of the reporters said. "What do you have to say to your fans, to—"

"No comment."

Alex shut the reporter down and plowed his way through the throng of people with Elijah in his wake.

Elijah beeped his truck unlocked, but the news crews had

the truck surrounded. They'd never be able to leave unless Alex made some sort of statement.

He wanted to acknowledge who he was, allowing room for Elijah in his public life.

He wanted to tell everyone to fuck off. Tell them that Elijah was someone special.

Tell the world he was gay.

But the letters wouldn't form into words and the words wouldn't form into sentences. He felt filleted in front of the world and everything he felt for the man he'd spent the most amazing night with was exposed to those who couldn't open their minds enough to understand it.

Or worse, didn't care to try.

Pressure came from all sides. Alex couldn't think, couldn't breathe. The questions whizzing by him one after the other—a flaming, crucifying, media shit-storm.

Then his eyes locked on the reporter from the night before —the woman who'd sat alone in the bleachers before the game. Her hair was pulled up in a messy ponytail, and her makeup appeared old and smudged.

And those clothes... Was she also wearing the same clothes that she'd worn the day before? Had she been the one who'd spent half the night in the tree behind Elijah's apartment filming them instead of running off to her husband like she claimed she would.

All of his anger, his sense of betrayal, he focused on her. She went to take a step back, but the jostling from the other reporters kept her in one place.

"You're a piece of work, you know that?"

"It wasn't me," she said, not into the microphone.

He plucked the microphone out of her hand. "Bullshit."

Turning his attention back to Elijah, he said, "Let's get out of here."

Not that he particularly wanted his ass reamed by a pissed-off Niko, but it beat a scandal-frenzied mob.

For once, the midday traffic was light. They couldn't turn on a radio station without news reports of the video. Alex's phone buzzed, and he glanced down to see his father's phone number flash on his screen. He hit ignore, and let the call go to voice-mail. This wasn't a conversation he wanted to have with his father. Not when he didn't have any of the answers.

After they arrived at Black Stallion, Rose met them both with a hug and led them back to Niko's office. She had one of those pained, sympathetic grimaces on her face. "I'll let Niko know you two are here. He should be finishing up with a scene any minute."

They sat beside each other in the leather chairs opposite Niko's desk. This didn't seem like the type of amenable conversation to have on the sofa. Elijah leaned forward in his chair, his forearms resting on his knees, his head in his hands. Elijah was about to lose a job. A job that he needed to put himself through school. If it wasn't for Alex, if it wasn't for his pseudo-celebrity, which leaned closer to infamous than famous, none of this would be happening.

Alex reached over and placed his hand on Elijah's shoulder, his thumb lightly brushing across the back of Elijah's neck. Elijah raised his head but didn't look over at Alex.

"I'm sorry," Alex said. "This is all my fault."

Elijah looked at him then, his brows drawn together. "How so?"

"If I was anybody else, no one would give a rat's ass who I saw or who I fucked, and Niko never would have found out."

"But you're not *anybody* else. I knew that from the beginning. I knew that when I agreed to drive us to the sports complex, and when I took you home, and when I let you do the things to me that I wanted you to do. Does this suck? Yeah, it sucks donkey balls. But I'm not the one who has to live with all the heat. You are."

Niko rapped his knuckles on the door jamb as he walked through the open door. Alex released Elijah's shoulder, and they both sat back in their chairs, bracing for the shouting, the yelling, the recriminations. But when Niko plopped into the chair behind his desk, there was no anger, no malice. Just disappointment.

"I guess you two know why you're here?"

"I don't think it's to congratulate us on our new viral video," Elijah said. One day, Alex would find Elijah's comment funny. But not today.

Niko didn't crack a smile. He leaned forward, his fingers steepled with his forearms resting on the edge of his desk. "I like you two. I really do. And the videos you two shot for Black Stallion have been nothing short of solid gold. But you two knew the rules going in. Black Stallion's reputation is something I can't take for granted. With all the hype, there's no way I can keep you two on."

"We understand. For the record, when I signed that paperwork," Alex said, "it was the truth. At least as much as I knew it. I never expected—"

Alex reached over and linked his fingers with Elijah's and gave Elijah's hand a squeeze. When he spoke again, he kept his gaze on Elijah when he said, "I never thought I could fall so hard so fast. Especially for a man." Then he looked back at Niko. "I'm not apologizing for that."

Elijah squeezed back and kept his gaze on the floor. The way some of the tension eased from Elijah's posture made Alex think that maybe some of his words had sunk in. Alex wanted Elijah to believe him. *Needed* Elijah to believe him.

Alex dropped Elijah's hand. With a finger under Elijah's

chin, Alex turned Elijah's face and pressed a kiss to his lips. A promise. "We're going to get through this. Trust me."

Elijah nodded. Alex could tell Elijah wanted to believe, but the expression on his face made it clear Alex had a long way to go to prove it to Elijah.

Niko cleared his throat, and Alex and Elijah turned their attention to him. "This goes against my normal policy, but by popular demand, I'm leaving your videos up. And I'm going to continue to allow you guys to earn your residuals."

Elijah blew out an audible breath. Alex's heightened anxiety eased a fraction.

"I've never let residuals continue before," Niko said. "This needs to be our dirty little secret. But as for a career at Black Stallion, you two are done. Any questions?"

That sounded like a dismissal. Alex stood. Elijah stood as well, reaching down and taking Alex's hand. Alex liked that. Liked that there was a public space where they could show affection and not worry about the reaction of the other people in the room. Would there ever be a time in his life that he could be this open with his sexuality everywhere?

What would hurt more? Losing his career or losing Elijah? And why the hell couldn't he keep both?

"I don't have any questions," Alex said.

"Thank you," Elijah added. "I appreciate your decision. And I apologize if we let the studio down."

They shook hands over the desk and Elijah preceded Alex to the door.

"To be clear," Niko said. Alex and Elijah stopped and turned. "As disappointed as I am that we'll no longer be working together, I'm happy for you two. Truly."

———

ELIJAH DIDN'T KNOW IF THE NEWS CREWS REMAINED CAMPED OUT in the parking lot of his apartment, so he didn't mind taking Alex to SFSC for his pitching session. They pulled around back and saw that Trevor had already dropped Alex's car off as Alex had asked.

Elijah drove toward the back door to drop Alex off when Alex said, "Do you mind parking?"

The parking lot at the back of the sports complex was nearly empty, and Elijah picked a spot and pulled his keys from the ignition. He stared at the complex's back door. Had it only been last night when he and Alex had slipped through that door? He remembered the way his stomach had tumbled and turned with sweet anticipation. How his hopes were as high as his libido.

Now not only had their private life gone viral, someone had made a GIF of Alex fucking him in the ass. Thanks went to Demetri for texting him that gem.

No one had laid a finger on Elijah, but he hadn't been this beat, battered, bruised since a group of kids had ganged up on him in high school and tried to beat the perceived fag out of him. And just when he thought his financial troubles were behind him, being booted out of Black Stallion would seriously put his ability to finish school at risk.

"Come in with me?" Alex asked. When Elijah glanced over, Alex added, "I want you to meet my pitching coach."

Elijah wanted to say no. Not because he didn't want to meet Alex's coach, but because it felt like Alex was throwing him a bone, and he didn't know if he had the balls to chase after it.

Alex is trying. You asked him to let you in. He's opened the door a crack. Are you going to slam it in his face? Or are you going to nut the hell up and shoulder your way through that door?

"Okay."

"Yeah?" The most amazed, surprised grin spread across

Alex's face. The type of grin that shoves the weight of the world off your shoulders for a moment and makes it easier to breathe.

"Yeah." Elijah climbed out of his truck, and Alex retrieved his equipment bag from the tail bed.

They came through the back door and down the long hallway. This time all the overhead lights were on. The crack of bats on balls echoed as pitching machines lobbed ball after ball after ball.

Alex nodded to some and ignored the stares of others. Elijah had hoped they had rented a cage in the far corner, out of the way of people coming and going. But, as luck would have it, the cage Alex's coach had chosen was at the intersection of two wide hallways, in full view of not only the batting cages, but the enormous two-story observation windows.

At the cage, Alex dropped his bag at his feet and stuck out his hand, first to an older Hispanic man dressed in athletic shorts and a Grizzlies' shirt, then to another man wearing leg guards and a chest protector.

"Elijah, this is my pitching coach, Fernando Gomez, and my good friend, Ethan Locke. Guys, this is Elijah Maddox. He's staying to watch."

Heat crept up the back of Elijah's neck. From the faked nonchalance on Ethan's and Gomez's faces, Alex didn't have to explain who Elijah was. Elijah shook both of their hands. "Nice to meet you."

Gomez handed Elijah a five-gallon bucket with a padded lid on top. "Have a seat and we'll get started."

The next twenty minutes consisted of Alex and Ethan throwing the ball in the cage as they slowly warmed up Alex's arm before Alex took the mound.

"Start him off with some fastballs," Gomez instructed Ethan.

A low-level buzz filled the sports complex. Once Alex started pitching, more people watched Alex than were working on their own training. Elijah shifted, feeling like the new curiosity at the zoo that no one quite knew what to make of.

Alex glanced up at the observation window, and Elijah followed his gaze. On the second level, at least three cameras had set up, but luckily, for now, management had kept the reporters to the public areas of the complex. How the hell had they found them so fast?

Elijah glanced around. Half a dozen people had their phones out, either tapping away with their thumbs or aiming the cameras in his and Alex's direction. Of course. All it took was one tweet, one post, one hashtag connected to Alex's name and the press came running.

To Alex, Gomez said, "Keep your head on straight, boy. Push all that crap out of your head. It's you and Ethan and that ball."

Alex blew out a deep breath and Elijah watched in amazement as the tension dropped from Alex's shoulders. He'd seen Alex do that several times in the video clips he'd found online of him pitching in the Minors. That deep breath. That roll of the shoulders. That laser focus of his eyes on the catcher's glove.

Gomez stepped over and handed Elijah the radar gun. "Hold that. And watch what your boy can do."

His boy.

Elijah liked the sound of that. A little too much.

Gomez clapped Elijah on the back, walked around the side of the cage, and stood there with his arms crossed over his chest as he watched Alex pitch. Gomez ran Alex through his paces— fastballs, curveballs, changeups, cutters, sliders. Each pitch more impressive than the other.

Elijah enjoyed hearing the whoosh of the ball as it sliced through the air, the slap of the ball against Ethan's glove, the occasionally muttered "fuck" when a fastball missed the web and hit Ethan's hand a little too hard.

"You're done," Gomez said at last.

Instead of the crowd inside the complex thinning out, more people crowded in.

Ethan stood, dropped his catcher's mask, and removed his chest protector, the back of his shirt soaked through. Alex came off the mound drenched as well, and Elijah tried not to think about last night when Alex's naked body had glistened with sweat. Ethan tossed him a hand towel and Alex mopped his face.

The door opened to the ground-floor reception area, and the low-level buzz turned into an eardrum numbing hum as the reporters poured into the aisle around Alex's cage.

Immediately, the tension returned to Alex's shoulders, and the satisfied smile of a job well done tumbled and fell. Elijah stepped toward the cage, wanting to be there by Alex's side, to support him, to be there for him, to let him know he wasn't alone in all this. But the look Alex shot him froze Elijah to the floor.

It wasn't a look of relief at seeing Elijah coming to his rescue, it was a flash of pure panic.

A flash that told Elijah that no matter what Alex had told him, Alex wasn't anywhere near ready to face the press with Elijah by his side. In the melee, as reporters jockeyed for position, Elijah fadded back, unnoticed and forgotten. He leaned a shoulder against a cinder block wall and watched from afar.

"Aren't you embarrassed? Do you think any club would be willing to sign you now? More importantly, should they?" One of the reporters from a major sports network asked Alex.

Alex glanced at the spot where Elijah had been sitting. Was that relief on his face at seeing Elijah gone? Elijah wanted to leave. He *should* leave. But something compelled him to stay.

"Embarrassed?" Alex's voice remained level, civil.

Elijah didn't know how Alex did it. Was Alex really that good at hiding his emotions? Or deep down did he really not care about Elijah?

"I've done nothing wrong. What two consenting adults do in the privacy of their home is no one's business. Unlike the person who took and released that video, I haven't broken any laws. I can't control what the clubs do. All I can do is work hard every day and improve my strength, my conditioning, my craft. Now if you'll excuse me, I need to go ice my arm."

If Alex had apologized or acted ashamed over what they'd done and what they'd shared, Elijah would have walked right out the door and not looked back, so he had to give Alex points for that, but Alex's lack of acknowledgment of Elijah's existence stung as if he'd been cleated in the heart.

Not a fatal wound, but it sure hurt like hell.

Alex and Ethan headed toward the locker rooms, Elijah straightened and went to follow them, but Alex caught his eye and gave a slight shake of his head.

Alex didn't want him there.

Was Alex protecting Elijah or pushing him away?

As much as Elijah didn't want to admit it, there didn't seem to be any room in Alex's life for him.

13

———

A MONTH LATER, ETHAN STOOD AT THE HEAD OF THE WEIGHT bench spotting Alex and counting his reps. "Has Gomez had any luck getting clubs interested in you?"

Trevor had an appointment so Alex had invited Ethan to come work out with him. Alex raised his eyes and grunted as he bench-pressed the barbell. Already on his third set, Alex's chest and triceps burned.

He really didn't want to talk about the lack of interest by the clubs, so he dropped the bar back to his chest and pushed it up again and repeated until finally Ethan hefted the bar from his outstretched hands and replaced it on the rack.

Ethan leaned on the bar and stared down at Alex flat on his back on the bench. "I'll take that as a no."

Alex sat up and shook out his arms as he waited for the sting of the lactic acid to diminish. "After the reporters showed up last month at the complex, they had shot enough video of me pitching to pique some renewed interest."

"So, maybe the video was a good thing? Got you some exposure you may not have received otherwise."

Alex picked up his towel and wiped his sweat off the bench.

"Maybe. But they're also spooked. None of the clubs want the kind of press that signing me would bring. That's not the kind of thing that sells season tickets."

"You dominating on the mound is what's going to sell tickets. You win games and your teammates and fans won't care who the hell you're sleeping with."

"I don't know. To my face, the managers say they don't have a problem with me having had sex with a man, but the fact no one is willing to make me an offer says otherwise."

They loaded more weight on the bar for Ethan. When Ethan took Alex's place on the bench, Alex stepped around to spot him.

"Keep your head down, keep working, keep grinding, it's gonna pay off. I know it will," Ethan said.

"That makes one of us."

"There comes a time in your life when you have to realize that baseball isn't everything. At least you have Elijah."

Says the man still playing professional baseball.

When Alex made a face, Ethan pushed the bar onto the rack and sat up. "I thought it was going well with you two."

Alex made a motion with his hand telling Ethan to get back to his workout. "It was—is," Alex corrected.

Ethan finished his first set of reps and Alex helped him guide the bar onto the rack. Ethan sat up again and leveled a gaze at him. One of those *get real* looks he'd shoot at the batters when they crowded the back of the box. "Is or was? Which one is it?"

"If you don't shut your trap, we're never going to get out of here today."

Ethan laid back down and grabbed hold of the bar, but before he lifted the barbell, he said, "Talk."

"Forget it," Alex said. "Guys like you wouldn't really understand."

"Guys like me?" Ethan pushed a lot of weight, and he had to talk between each rep. His arms began to shake under the strain, but he kept going.

"Straight guys," Alex clarified.

Ethan got quiet. He finished that set of reps, rested, then started on another. Alex considered the conversation over. Ethan pushed the barbell up one last time, and Alex helped set it on the rack. Exertion reddened Ethan's face, and a vessel throbbed at his temple.

Ethan reached for his towel and wiped the sweat from his face. "Maybe I know more about what you're talking about than you think."

Alex paused with his water bottle halfway to his mouth, his head thrown back as his eyes shifted to Ethan. "What are you trying to say?"

"I'm saying I understand what you're going through." Ethan rubbed a hand across the back of his neck and glanced around the gym. There were a few women on the treadmills. A couple of bodybuilder dudes in the corner by the dumbbells, but everyone had earbuds in, and no one was paying them a bit of attention. "What I'm saying is: I'm gay."

Water went down Alex's trachea, and he coughed and sputtered sending water all over the mats at his feet. "What the fuck?"

Ethan had a self-deprecating grin on his face. "Surprise."

"Why the hell didn't you say anything?"

"It's not something I tell people. Ever." Ethan's eyes nearly went lethal. Alex had never seen him that serious, even with need-to-win games on the line. "And I mean, *ever*."

Alex raised his hands in surrender. "Hey, man, no one is going to hear that shit from me." Alex pointed to the bench. "You going to finish your last set?"

Ethan shook his head. "Naw, I think I'm done here." He

sounded lost. Almost defeated. This from the man who'd been called up at the end of the season and would be playing in the majors the next year. What did Ethan have to be dejected about? His professional career was taking off.

They gathered their towels and their water bottles and headed for the showers. Alex couldn't believe the bomb Ethan had dropped on him.

"So how do you balance who you are with the game? You've flown completely under the radar. No one knows. No one suspects. How did you manage that?"

"It's called discretion. Something you seem to be unfamiliar with," Ethan said with a laugh.

"So, what? You got some guy chained in a sex sling in your apartment that no one knows about? Someone who only comes out under cover of darkness to fuck and suck, like some kind of gay vampire?"

By the scale, Ethan stopped and glanced around again. They were alone. It would be another hour at least before the after-work crowd started stumbling in. "It's not like that."

Ethan had a reputation for positivity. A positivity that seemed to drain from his body in front of Alex's eyes.

"You don't have anybody in your life." It wasn't a question. Alex could read it in the slump of Ethan's shoulders and the way he wouldn't meet Alex' gaze.

"Not really."

Something in the way Ethan said those two words piqued Alex's interest. "But you have your eye on somebody." The way Ethan glanced up at him, defeat in his eyes, Alex knew he was right. "A teammate?"

"No." Ethan glanced away. "It's stupid, really. Nothing can come of it."

"A coach?"

Ethan turned his back and headed for the locker room again.

Alex had to jog to keep up. "What do you do?" Alex really wasn't trying to pry. He was trying to understand.

No way Ethan went through life celibate. They'd been teammates for chrissake. They'd shared rooms on the road together. Hell, he'd covered for Ethan many times when he hadn't made it back to the room until right before the team loaded up on the team buses.

"Anonymous hookups?"

Ethan shushed him as he shouldered his way into the locker room. When they found the locker room empty, Ethan said, "I used the apps, mostly. Until some dude recognized me. After that, it wasn't worth the risk."

"Then what did you do?"

"I hired escorts."

Ethan could have said anything, and it wouldn't have surprised Alex as much as his real answer. "You pay people for sex?"

Ethan laughed at that and patted Alex on the back. "I don't pay them to fuck me. I pay them for their discretion and to leave once we're done. But this isn't about me. I just... I just wanted you to know that I understand. I'd give my left nut to have what you and Elijah have."

"You don't have to give up one of your balls," Alex said, "apparently it's only your career you have to sacrifice."

"Yeah, well, I'll let you blaze that trail, I'm not ready to do that yet."

They both stripped and showered off, remaining quiet as they dressed and packed their dirty clothes into their gym bags. Ethan had taken a huge risk coming out to him, and Alex now felt obliged to set the record straight about him and Elijah.

"I don't think you want what Elijah and I have," Alex said. Ethan shot him a cursory look as he closed his locker and spun the dial. "I mean, he's great. He's thoughtful, he's giving, he's funny, and the sex... The sex is off the charts. And honestly, I could really see building a life with him. But every time I think we're getting closer, I feel him pulling away."

"Come to think of it, maybe I don't want what you have."

This should be good.

Alex crossed his arms over his chest.

"I had a friend once tell me that relationships can't bloom without light. The closet is an ugly, dark place to live your life. Take it from someone who knows. Elijah must really love you if he's willing to put up with you treating him the way you do."

Alex put a hand to the center of Ethan's chest and shoved him back into the lockers with a bang. "What the hell are you talking about?"

Ethan glanced down at Alex's hand then back up again. Anger didn't flood Ethan's gaze, just pity. Which pissed Alex off even more.

"You don't know anything about our relationship."

"I know that you've barely acknowledged he exists. I know when you're out at the bar with your friends, you treat him like a buddy, not someone you take to your bed. I know you two sneak around, meet in hotel rooms as if what you're doing is wrong."

"Says the guy paying for escorts."

"Says the guy *not* in a relationship. Says the guy *not* leading some poor schmuck around on a leash promising something he can't deliver. Tell me, Einstein, how long do you think Elijah's going to put up with your bullshit?"

"Why are you taking this so personally?"

It was Ethan's turn to shove Alex into the lockers, his wide hand landed like a battering ram to Alex's chest. "Because Elijah is a great guy, and you're fucking up a good thing."

Alex knocked Ethan's hand away. "That's not really any of your business."

"You're a fucking piece of work, man."

Ethan blew out a breath and rolled his eyes. The tension dropped from Ethan's shoulders, and the anger drained from his face. Ethan was the type of guy who exploded, but he wasn't the kind of guy who held grudges. As soon as the dust cleared, he went on like nothing ever happened.

They shouldered their gym bags and headed for their vehicles as the parking lot started filling up. Ethan beeped his car unlocked and tossed his gym bag in the back seat. "I'll see you at The Night Owl tonight?"

Alex tossed his own bag into the trunk of his car. "I haven't decided."

The words Ethan had spoken not five minutes before echoed in his head. *How long is Elijah going to put up with your bullshit?*

"It's a celebration for Elijah, and you don't know if you're going?" Ethan couldn't hide the exasperation in his voice. Then again, maybe he hadn't tried. "Dude, you're such a dick. Hopefully, Elijah is smart enough to come to his senses and dump your sorry ass."

———

"Is Alex coming?" Demetri asked as he poured Elijah a glass of beer from the pitcher in the center of the table.

They were at The Night Owl bar, one street off campus, celebrating the contract Elijah had signed to become a brand ambassador for *King Dong*. The money had come when Elijah had been contemplating giving up his apartment and moving in with a friend and sleeping on their couch.

Elijah glanced at his watch. It was almost nine o'clock. Almost everyone else he'd invited had arrived already. Almost everyone, except Alex. Elijah's chest felt hollowed, as if Alex had reached in and scooped out his heart. As much as he wanted a relationship with Alex, as good as it was when they were together, he couldn't go on like this. It hurt too damn much.

"He probably had a pitching session that ran late," Demetri said.

Maybe. Elijah had learned he couldn't always count on Alex to show up in public at the same place he'd be. Elijah had his friends there—Demetri, Shannon from the life drawing class, guys from his rec baseball team, even Trevor was there.

The door to the bar opened, and all heads at their table turned. Ethan walked in and Elijah got his hopes up. But the door behind Ethan closed without Alex slipping in behind him.

Don't ask about Alex. Don't ask about Alex. Don't ask about Alex.

Elijah stood as Ethan approached the table and stuck out his hand. "Hey, man, glad you could make it."

Ethan pulled him in for a one-arm hug and a slap on the back. "Congrats, man. Thanks for the invite."

Ethan had a stiff, forced smile on his face, as he glanced around and noticed Alex wasn't there. Elijah pushed out his own synthetic smile, the effort monumental. He'd give Alex another fifteen minutes. Twenty tops. And if he didn't show by then...

Ethan helped himself to the beer, turned a chair around, and sat, striking up a conversation with one of the guys from Elijah's team who usually played catcher. They started talking about pitch counts and pitch selection, and Elijah's attention drifted.

Shannon had commandeered the seat beside him, her tongue darting out and licking salt from the rim of her margarita glass before she took a sip.

She had a thing for him and she hadn't been shy about letting him know. As the night wore on, and the fifteen minutes turn to twenty, twenty turned to sixty, and Alex hadn't shown up, Ethan started to wonder why he shouldn't take Shannon up on what she had offered on more than one occasion.

After all, Alex had been clear he couldn't make Elijah any promises. Elijah was a patient man, but he wasn't a doormat.

That late on a Friday night in a college town bar, it was almost impossible to hear over the laughing and the raised voices and the music pumping out of the speakers. He had to lean in when Shannon said, "I thought you were going to show us the pictures from your *King Dong* photo shoot."

No one else had asked to see the photos, and he hadn't been too keen on flashing them around, but Demetri and Shannon were different. They'd seen him naked for hours on end. He had zero to hide. Elijah pulled out his phone as Demetri and Shannon leaned in.

Shannon scooted her chair closer and looped an arm through his, her breast smooshing up against his triceps. He had to ease a hand down and adjust himself in his jeans. She really was a beautiful woman. Sweet, considerate, the type of woman any man would be happy to take to their bed.

Why shouldn't Elijah take her to his?

He could use a little sex, a little connection, without the self-recrimination, the shame of letting someone treat him as *less than* the way Alex sometimes did. He'd told Alex he would give him some time to sort their relationship with respect to Alex's career, but in the time that he'd given Alex, Elijah had done all the giving, and frankly, he had nothing left to offer a relationship that he couldn't see going anywhere.

Elijah thumbed to the folder of photos the *King Dong* photographer had sent him and slowly shuffled through them for Demetri and Shannon to see.

"Don't get me wrong," Shannon said, "I love the way you look when you're completely nude." She should know. She'd been staring at his junk all semester. "But there's something totally hot about seeing you in these jockstraps. What do you think, Demetri?"

"They're fucking hot." Demetri's voice came out thick, but ever since that first time Elijah had turned down Demetri's offer, Demetri had been man enough to take no for an answer and hadn't pushed their friendship boundary. "The lighting really emphasizes your muscles and highlights the veins in your arms."

Elijah flipped to another picture, and Shannon took the phone from his hands and pinched the screen, enlarging the photo. "Holy moly." His crotch filled the screen of his smartphone. "Did they have you—" Shannon made a jacking-off motion with her hand.

Elijah laughed. He loved a woman who wasn't afraid to say what was in her head, no matter how inappropriate. And it made him wonder again what it would be like to take her to his bed.

Before he could answer, a hand came down on his shoulder. He knew who that hand belonged to even before he scooted his chair back and glanced up at its owner.

"Can I talk to you a minute?" Alex bobbed his chin toward the back hallway where they would have a modicum of privacy. It almost pissed Elijah off more that Alex had come to his party late than if he hadn't come at all. With the mood Elijah was in, all he wanted to say was fuck off.

Elijah took Shannon's hand and stood. "It'll have to wait. We were headed to the bar to get a couple more pitchers of beer. Weren't we?" Elijah gave Shannon's hand a please-play-along squeeze.

"Yeah. We'll be right back." Shannon tugged on his hand and led him toward the bar.

They edged in between a couple of people and Elijah raised his hand to the bartender and held up two fingers. The bartender acknowledged him with a nod.

"Kiss me." Shannon eased closer, her body pressed up

against his, dropping her hand and resting it on his ass. "You want to make him jealous, don't you?"

Elijah didn't dare look back at their table. He knew Alex was staring at him by the way his skin prickled under Alex's heated gaze. Trying to make Alex jealous was a childish, assholery thing to do, but that didn't stop Elijah from leaning in and pressing his lips against hers.

Her mouth immediately opened, her tongue darting in. He tasted the salt, the tang from the tequila, and the sweetness of the triple sec. But beneath all of that was a sweetness that was all Shannon.

The crowd around the bar jostled them, but that didn't keep him from taking the kiss deeper, of running his hands down to the curve of her hip and snugging her up against him.

A few months ago, Shannon's kisses would have made his dick hard, but something was... off. Her perfume smelled too flowery. Her body felt too soft. Her sighs sounded too high pitched.

And, damn it, he craved the scrape of stubble against his skin.

The rebellious part of him wanted to take her home and fuck her. And as much as she was into him, that would be an dick move, especially when he'd be closing his eyes and wishing he was screwing Alex the whole time.

He broke the kiss.

What the fuck was he playing at?

"Your beer," the bartender said as he slid the two pitchers onto the bar top.

Elijah reached into his wallet and threw cash on the bar. "Thanks, man."

They each took a pitcher in hand. Before they left their spot at the bar, Shannon leaned in and whispered in his ear, "My offer stands. In case you ever change your mind. No pressure."

"Thanks. You know, any other time," he lied.

"Hey, I get it. No hard feelings."

They turned, and almost doused Alex with their beer. Alex stripped the pitcher out of Elijah's hand and handed it to Shannon. Alex had a scowl on his face, one Elijah had only seen on video clips when batters had given him lip from the batter's box.

To Shannon, Alex said, "I need a word. You won't mind taking these to the table, would you?"

"I mind," Elijah said. "My friends are waiting."

"Please?" Alex's voice softened, making Elijah feel like an asshole. "This will only take a minute."

Shannon gave Elijah a wink and left with the beer. Alex clamped a proprietary hand on Elijah's shoulder and steered him toward the back hallway. Elijah shook off Alex's hand.

A couple of women squeezed by them on their way to the restrooms, but otherwise, he and Alex were about as alone as they could be in public.

Alex crowded into Elijah's personal space, and Elijah retreated until his back bumped against the ridges of the corrugated steel walls. Alex's blue eyes had turned that dark, turbulent color that made seasoned sea captains head for a sheltered port. "What were you doing kissing her?"

If the baseball thing didn't work out for Alex, he should get a job in comedy because he was hi-*fucking*-larious. "I never heard you call dibs. The only time you call me anymore is when you want to meet me at some sleazy motel to dip your dick in my ass."

The mask of jealousy and possessiveness on Alex's face dropped away, leaving only hurt. Guess Alex did have a heart buried in there after all.

"That's not the only reason I call you. You know that."

"Tell me why you call then? Go ahead. I'm listening." Only Elijah wasn't. He couldn't. Not when the blood roared past his eardrums as if someone had cranked up the flow at Niagara Falls.

Alex swallowed hard, his mouth opening and closing before any words could tumble out.

Well, if Alex couldn't find the words, Elijah had plenty to spare. "We've made no promises to each other. The *one* promise you made me, the one where you promised to find a way to fit me into your public life..."

Elijah's voice cracked. God, he fucking hated it that Alex had the power to ripsaw his emotions. Elijah cleared his throat. "You've broken that. Don't—"

Alex grabbed a handful of Elijah's shirt and pressed him against the wall, the corrugation digging into Elijah's shoulder blades. Alex's mouth crashed down on Elijah's, hard, hot, hungry.

Elijah wanted to kick himself for not putting up even a token resistance, but the kiss made his heart trip, his knees weak, and his head search for excuses, because as wounded and disappointed as Elijah was in Alex, Elijah knew there was so much more between them than just the physical.

Alex wouldn't have the ability to strip him to his soul with one kiss if there wasn't.

What made it worse, was that Elijah knew what he'd demanded of Alex had been too much, too soon. But he was asking because he'd finally come to a point in his life where he'd realized he was worth it.

Alex deepened the kiss, his erection pressing into Elijah's hip when he shifted and all Elijah wanted to do was toss Alex into the back of his truck and haul him to the nearest anonymous pay-by-the-hour motel, crawl under his skin, and fuck some sense into him.

But in the long, sordid history of mankind, sex had never solved anything.

"Stop," Elijah managed between kisses.

Alex must not have heard because all he did was shift his focus and start nipping at the scruff on Elijah's chin.

"Stop," Elijah said again, with more conviction and a hand on Alex's chest.

Alex took a step back, a deep grove formed between his brows, and a growing uncertainty showed in his eyes. "You really mean that?"

Elijah didn't.

Though he should.

He really, *really* should.

But did Alex think that he was that easy? That too far gone that all Alex had to do was get Elijah hot and horny and he'd fall into bed with him, their argument forgotten?

Fuck that.

And fuck Alex.

Or rather, *not* fuck Alex.

Elijah gave Alex a shove, with all of his frustration and anger and bruised feelings behind it. It knocked Alex back into the opposite wall, the shock and surprise gave Elijah time to close the gap and get into Alex's face.

Elijah drilled his finger into Alex's sternum as he spoke. "I'm done with this game. I'm not interested in being your shameful, secret piece on the side. I refuse to stay tucked away in your pathetic little closet. There's not enough room in there for the both of us."

The women came out of the restroom and passed behind him, giving them both the side eye.

"Eli—"

Elijah wasn't finished giving Alex what he had coming. "You're not fooling anyone. The proof is on that viral video. Yet you deny who you are."

"I'm not denying anything."

"Oh no, that's right. You're not denying anything because you don't have to. Because you refuse to be seen alone with me in public. Which is the same fucking thing. Deny me all you want." Elijah pointed toward the rest of the bar. "Everyone out there already knows the score except you."

"It's not like that."

Elijah got right in Alex's face again, their noses nearly touching. "Prove it." He took Alex's hand in his and started tugging him toward the tables. "Go back out there and kiss me in front of everyone."

Elijah came up short when Alex couldn't be budged.

Conflict cut harsh lines in Alex's expression. As much as he might want to do as Elijah asked, he couldn't make himself take that first step.

"Yeah." Elijah dropped Alex's hand. "That's what I thought. One of these days you're gonna want to stop living a lie and live your life with some fucking integrity. Live your truth. Just don't call me when you do."

Elijah turned on his heel. A sound escaped the back of Alex's throat, but Elijah refused to look back because if he did, he'd try to take back every word he'd said, even if he'd spoken nothing but the truth.

As Elijah walked back to his table of friends, he knew another truth: It was time to move on with his life.

Demetri sat alone at their table. Elijah glanced around. The other guys had spread out. Some were playing darts. Some were crowded around a pool table with a giggly pack of co-eds.

"Everything all right?" Demetri asked when Elijah picked up his warm beer and slugged the whole thing back.

"Why wouldn't it be?"

Shannon sidled up against Elijah. "There you are. I was about to send in a SEAL team to come to your rescue."

Elijah needed a rescue all right. He put his arm around Shannon's waist and said, "I think it's time for me to leave."

He shook Demetri's hand. "I appreciate you coming."

"Sure thing."

He squeezed Shannon's hip. "You want to come with?"

Shannon was a grown woman who knew the score. He wouldn't be using her any more than she'd be using him.

"I'd like that," she said.

Elijah took her by the hand, noticing the way his hand engulfed hers instead of how Alex's hand engulfed his. And she didn't have those callouses on her fingers from throwing baseballs.

He pushed those unsettling differences out of his mind and said goodbye to Trevor and the rest of the guys and thanked them for coming.

As they pushed through the front door, Shannon squeezed up against him, settling under his arm, her giggles sweet and high pitched—not that low grumble of Alex's that always seemed to hit Elijah low in his gut making the blood rush south and making him want to pin Alex down and do nasty, lascivious things to him.

At his truck, she pressed Elijah against his door and straddled one of his legs, her hands snaking beneath his shirt and fanning across his lower abdomen. He waited for the flutter of his abdominal muscles beneath her touch, a flutter that never came.

Instead, he couldn't get Alex's expression out of his head when he'd told Alex not to call him if he ever got his shit together—regret, defeat, rejection, betrayal, all warred for prominence, but it had been what Elijah could only describe as anguish that had won out at the end.

Elijah must have interpreted that wrong. He didn't have that kind of power over a guy like Alex. His gut twisted, and it wasn't with desire from the way Shannon expertly licked and sucked her way up his neck.

Fuck. He couldn't do this.

Because you're hopelessly stuck on Alex, no matter what you'd said to him in the bar.

No. Because it wouldn't be fair to Shannon.

He'd already led her on enough and treating a woman that way, no matter how conflicted he was, was a shitty thing to do. And he had to stop it before he wrecked their friendship.

He placed his hands on her hips and pushed her back until her crotch wasn't rubbing up against his thigh and her teeth weren't nibbling on his earlobe.

"Not gonna happen, is it?" she asked. He couldn't detect any frustration or animosity mixed with the wistfulness.

"I'm sorry, I—"

"Don't be sorry. I hope one day I can find someone who feels about me the same way you feel about him." His hands dropped as she stepped back. She stuck her hand out for him to shake. "Friends?"

He accepted her hand. "Friends."

As she backed away, she added, "Don't lock and barricade that door." She tilted her head toward the bar, indicating Alex. "Leave it open a crack. At least for now. He strikes me as a smart guy. Maybe he'll come around."

Elijah didn't dare hope. "Drive safe."

He opened his driver's side door, watching Shannon walk away, making sure she made it to her car safely before he left. Shannon beeped her car unlocked as the front door of the bar flew open and banged against the wall behind it, spitting Alex out. "Elijah, wait!"

———

ONE OF THESE DAYS YOU'RE GONNA WANT TO STOP LIVING A LIE.

Just don't call me when you do.

Elijah's words echoed in Alex's head as he watched an amazing man walk out of his life.

...stop living a lie...

...stop living a lie...

Just don't call me when you do.

Alex leaned over, bracing his hands on his knees, the wall behind him keeping him from falling.

If he'd had any doubts before, he didn't have any now. It was over.

He tried to straighten, but there was a dull pain in his chest, his heart bruised. He couldn't catch his breath. It was as if a bat had slammed into his chest. Dark spots danced in the corner of his vision, and he stared down the hall to the bar's entrance where he could have sworn that he'd seen Elijah dragging Shannon out by her hand.

It was better this way.

Bullshit.

He could concentrate on his career without the constant attention and pressure from the media.

You're such a scrote.

Alex leaned his head back against the wall and ran his hands down his face. He would get through this.

Someone clapped him on the shoulder. Alex opened his eyes. Demetri stood before him, a sour scowl of disapproval—or was that disdain?—on his face.

"I get that love can be messy, complicated, and brutal, but you're an idiot if you let that man get away."

Love? "No one said anything about love."

Demetri laughed in his face. "You wouldn't be standing here looking like someone had reached in and yanked your insides out if watching him walk out that door with a woman hadn't gutted you."

"You don't know what you're talking about."

Demetri held his hands up and backed down the hallway towards the men's room, the pity caked thickly on his face like some sort of mask.

Alex glanced back at the door where Elijah had walked out. If this was love, he didn't want any part of it. It hurt like hell.

Go get him.

His feet started walking of their own volition. By the time he'd made it down the hallway, he'd broken into a jog. He could make this right. It wasn't too late.

Please don't let it be too late.

Alex burst outside, the door banging off the wall, and slapping him in his pitching shoulder, but he didn't care.

He skidded to a stop and scanned the dark parking lot. A car alarm beeped, and he watched Shannon climb into the driver's seat of her car. Three aisles over, he spotted Elijah getting into his truck.

"Elijah, wait!"

Elijah froze. From that distance in the dark, Alex couldn't read Elijah's expression. What remained of Alex's heart kicked and punched at his sternum as they stared at each other across the parking lot.

Then whatever had kept Elijah rooted in place, broke. Instead of moving toward Alex, Elijah calmly climbed into his truck, closed the door, and drove off without so much as a tap of his brakes.

Alex had fucked up. Big time.

14

———

The media room at Fink Field, home of the Hawks' Double-A baseball team, buzzed with activity. Alex sat in the middle of a long table with the Hawks' coach, Declan King on one side and Fernando Gomez on the other.

Under normal circumstances, re-signing a Double-A pitcher before spring training wouldn't garner much attention, but after all of Alex's time in the spotlight recently, Coach King knew that there would have to be a press conference to handle all the media questions at once.

Alex sipped at his bottle of water, scanning the gathering crowd. Most were media, but former teammates stood against the back wall, offering their support. He nodded at them.

And, of course, Trevor was in amongst them, grinning like a fool.

But the one guy Alex wanted there most, wasn't.

This was the day Alex had worked so hard for. All those hours in rehab, in the gym, with his pitching coach in the cages, it all culminated at this moment.

The moment he re-signed with the Grizzlies' Minor League affiliate, the Hawks.

One step closer to a spring training invite. And hopefully, one step closer to another shot at the big leagues.

And all Alex wanted to do was duck out the back door and hightail it to Black Stallion where Demetri had let it slip that Elijah was doing another brand ambassador photo shoot for *King Dong*.

Luckily, he had a plan and Demetri had agreed to help.

He'd wanted to be there for Elijah, even though Elijah had wanted no contact since the night the month before when Alex had let him walk out of the bar without him.

He'd tried calling. Texting. Emailing. But the calls and texts went unanswered. His emails bounced. Knocking on Elijah's apartment door when Elijah's truck was in the parking lot, proved fruitless.

A couple of days ago, he'd waited outside Demetri's classroom hoping to catch Elijah as he came out after a life drawing class. Alex had been leaning against the bank of floor-to-ceiling windows, the sunlight streaming in, when Elijah came through the door and turned in his direction, his focus on his phone.

Then Elijah glanced up, saw Alex standing there and changed his direction. Alex hadn't chased after him.

Alex would have wholly given up if it hadn't been for Demetri telling Alex how grumpy and out of sorts Elijah had been since their fight.

But there was only so much Alex could do if Elijah refused to talk to him. If Alex kept it up, Elijah might get sick and tired of seeing his face everywhere he turned and drive to the nearest police station to file a restraining order.

Tonight was his last shot.

As long as Demetri didn't let him down.

———

"WHY ARE YOU TURNING IN AT FINK FIELD?" ELIJAH ASKED Demetri.

They were on their way back from Elijah's photo shoot with *King Dong* where they'd used one of the sets at Black Stallion Studios.

The New York skyline set.

The whole time they'd been shooting, Elijah kept eyeing the fake office window, remembering how the cold glass on his back felt as Alex had pressed him up against it and got down on his knees and sucked him off.

Probably one of his most memorable blow jobs, and it had nothing to do with him having downloaded and watched it over and over again while he'd jacked off.

At the studio, everywhere he'd looked reminded him of Alex, of that first thrill of attraction, the electric nerves, the spine-tingling orgasms.

He wouldn't give up those two weekends at Black Stallion for the world.

He also wished they'd never happened.

He'd been financially broke, but he hadn't been miserable. Or sleepless. Or second guessing everything he'd done or said in the past few months. Poor Cat had to work her makeup magic to cover the bags under his eyes.

And if he didn't get his shit together and concentrate on his classes, he'd be lucky to graduate come May.

"*Demetri.*"

Demetri pulled into a parking space behind one of the local news crew vans and cut the engine. He turned in his seat. "Look—"

"You had this planned all along, didn't you?"

At least the bastard had the decency to look chagrined.

"That story you spun about us carpooling to Black Stallion because you had a meeting with Niko anyway, was that all a lie?"

"More of an innocent embellishment."

"I'm calling bullshit." Elijah reached in his pocket for his phone. "Alex put you up to this, didn't he?"

Demetri grabbed Elijah's phone, but Elijah wouldn't let go.

"What are you doing?" Demetri had a tight grip.

"I'm calling an Uber."

"Would you hear me out?"

After a beat, Elijah nodded, and Demetri let go of the phone.

"Yes, Alex asked me to bring you here."

Motherfucker. "You're *my* friend. You're supposed to be on *my* side."

"I am on your side. If I wasn't, Alex couldn't have talked me into this."

Unbelievable.

Elijah popped the door latch and thumbed open the rideshare app, but the seatbelt brought him up short giving Demetri a chance to put a hand on his forearm and stop him from leaving.

"Go in there. When it's over, if you never want to see him again, he's promised to stay out of your life. Deal?"

How do you expect to get over Alex, if he refuses to go away?

Go in so he wouldn't have to wonder if he'd see Alex around every corner he turned? That almost sounded like a deal too good to pass up.

If it meant he had to watch the stupid press conference for Alex's re-signing to get Alex out of his life once and for all, he would.

And, yeah, as much as he tried to avoid all things Alex, he'd have to have gone full ostrich-head-in-the-sand mode to have not found out that the Hawks' had re-signed him.

To have not read about it online.

To have not watched all the news reports about it.

To have not stalked the Minor League Baseball pages about it.

You're fucking pathetic.

Elijah eyed the hand Demetri held out and shook it. "Deal."

By the time they slipped quietly into the back of the room, the press conference had already started. The constant strobe of camera flashes was bracing enough to trigger seizures.

Alex sat at a table dressed in a Hawks' jersey and baseball cap flanked by Gomez and one of the coaches from the Hawks' organization.

At the moment Elijah entered the room, Alex's gaze flicked to him, and for a blip of time, Alex's public smile turned heated and intimate. That satisfied turn of Alex's lip Elijah had only witnessed after Alex had given him a good pounding.

It hit Elijah the way he imagined that first hit of heroin feels like as it slams into an addict who'd just thrown away years of sobriety.

It hit like he was home.

He couldn't do this.

Elijah took a step toward the door, but Demetri clamped a hand on his shoulder, pinning him in place.

A buzz of murmurs zipped around the room. People glanced back at Elijah, and the unease crawled under his skin as if it were a living, breathing entity.

Elijah was afraid to smile back at Alex, not only because of the attention it would garner, but because he feared it would show his vulnerability and how truly gone he was for this man.

In the middle of Coach King's answer to a reporter's question, Elijah took his eyes off Alex and tuned back in.

"The club should never have let him go," Coach King said. "But that's baseball. Alex's recovery post Tommy John surgery fell well behind the curve. Management must make the best decisions they can with respect to the budget and the information they have on hand. Sometimes you make a mistake. And sometimes, like today, a team is lucky enough to rectify that mistake."

King patted Alex on the back. Alex grinned like a man about to get the keys to the kingdom, his chest swelled out with pride.

When King called on the next reporter, the woman asked, "What do you think it means for your team that you'll be adding a man like Alex to the roster?"

The question hung there in the silence. A silent stink bomb that permeated every corner of the room. People cleared their throats, glanced down, and shifted from foot to foot, though everyone had known the subject of Alex's sexuality would come up.

King gave Alex's shoulder a squeeze and leaned into the microphone. "A man like Alex?" He stared at the reporter for a long second, then another. "You mean a pitcher, correct?"

The reporter stammered but King talked over her. "It means we'll win games. That's what it means."

"What if his teammates have a problem with him?" That from a guy near the back. Now that the subject of Alex's sexuality had been broached, it was like the little Dutch boy had pulled his finger out of the dike, the inappropriate questions flooding out.

"My door is always open. My players know that. They have a problem, we can have a conversation about their concerns. If they can't get past Alex's personal life then, yeah, it's going to be a problem."

King let that sink in. Alex's face became stoic, and he adjusted and readjusted his cap as if it no longer fit well. King glanced at Alex and added, "For them, not Alex."

Addressing the room at large again, King said, "If my players can't be an adult in the locker room and on the field, I'm happy to release them from their contract. Trust me, there are plenty of extremely talented young men out there who would jump at the opportunity to take the empty slot on the roster."

As the murmurs died down, King called on a reporter near the front.

"This question is for Alex," the reporter said. Alex scooted his chair closer to the table and the mic. "There's been a lot of speculation about you over the past few months. Most of it met with 'no comments.' For the record, how would you label your sexual orientation?"

Before Alex could speak, Coach King cut in. "What does that have to do with baseball?"

"It's okay."

Alex didn't shrink from the question the way Elijah had expected he would. He sat straighter, bearing the confidence of a man approaching the mound knowing he was about to strike out the side. "I'd like to answer."

Elijah glanced at Demetri. Demetri had some screwed up enigmatic expression on his face that gave away absolutely nothing.

Alex cleared his throat into the microphone and Elijah returned his focus to the front of the room.

"I'm going to have to answer your question with a question." Alex's eyes fell away from the reporter and found Elijah at the back of the room. "What do you call it when you think of someone first thing in the morning and the last thing at night? When you can't wait to hear their voice, their laugh?"

Gradually, people turned, following Alex's gaze.

"What do you call it," Alex continued, "when you want to put a smile on their face? When they're the first one you want to tell about the good things, and the one you want to run to when things go bad?"

The heat burned up Elijah's neck and settled in his cheeks,

but his embarrassment paled in comparison to the way Alex's words picked up those scattered pieces of his heart and started putting them back where they belonged, piece by broken piece.

By now, not only had everyone turned toward Elijah, but the crowd had parted, like some modern-day parting of the Red Sea shit, and Elijah now had a direct line of sight to Alex.

But Alex wasn't finished. "What do you call it when you pour your heart and soul out to someone and hope like hell it's not too late and that they can forgive you for all your bullshittery?"

The room remained silent. Alex pulled the microphone closer. "That wasn't a rhetorical question."

The reporter who'd asked him for a label stammered. "Uh... love?"

Alex grinned, but not at the reporter. At Elijah. "There you have it then."

Holy shit. Alex loved him?

Where had all the oxygen gone in the room? It was there a second ago. Then... poof. Elijah swayed, and Demetri held him by the back of the neck, grounding him. Elijah scrubbed a shaky hand across his jaw and finally drew in a breath.

Alex popped the wireless microphone out of the stand and stood. "The short, *very personal,* answer to your question is that I'm gay."

Alex didn't hesitate. It rolled off his tongue as if he were telling the reporters his shoe size. Size thirteen by the way. If anyone asked Elijah how he'd found that out, he'd flat out lie.

Alex skimmed around the end of the table and walked toward Elijah, the camera flashes coming fast and furious and the video cameras getting more up close and personal than Vin at Black Stallion ever had.

"I'm gay," he said again, maybe for those in the back not paying attention. "And I'm stupidly, hopelessly in love with a man who would be insane to take me back, but I'm asking."

Alex stopped in front of Elijah and lowered the mic. Reaching up, he cupped Elijah's cheek, lowering his voice when he said, "I love you, Elijah. What do you say? Will you give me another chance? I swear it will be a decision you won't regret."

Their relationship had begun in front of the camera. Seemed fitting it would continue that way as well. Elijah swallowed, but that did nothing to dislodge the baseball-sized lump in his throat, so he nodded, holding himself together.

Cumming on camera was so much sexier than crying.

"Yeah?" Alex's eyes lit, and it wasn't from the additional artificial lighting.

"Yeah," Elijah managed.

Alex ducked his head—*and holy fuck yes*—kissed him in front of their friends, his teammates, his coach, the reporters, the cameras... the world.

And not a chaste peck on the lips. A deep dive. Tongues and teeth and heartfelt promises.

When Alex finally broke the kiss, he wrapped his arm around Elijah's shoulder, holding him tight against his body. He turned to the room at large. "Does that answer everyone's questions?"

———

AFTER THE PRESS CONFERENCE, ALEX COULDN'T GET ELIJAH AWAY from all the cameras and reporters fast enough. On the way to his apartment, they only stopped long enough to pick up an order of Chinese food.

Alex unlocked his front door and ushered Elijah into the kitchen where they dumped the bags of food on the kitchen island.

Elijah started unpacking the bags. Alex wanted food, but he wanted Elijah more. He walked up behind Elijah, took the two cartons of food out of his hand and placed them back on the counter.

Elijah reached into the bag and pulled out the condiments. "Hey, you were supposed to put them on the table."

Alex spanned his hands on the bar on either side of Elijah, pressing his hips against the hard muscle of Elijah's ass.

"You trying to tempt me?" The way Elijah's voice dropped two registers raised goosebumps on Alex's flesh.

Jesus Christ. Alex ran his hands under Elijah's shirt and spanned them across his belly. "Do you know how long I've wanted you in my arms again?"

He nipped at the juncture where Elijah's neck met his shoulder and soothed the bite with the caress of his tongue. Elijah smelled of fresh soap with a hint of whatever oil he must have slathered on himself for the photo shoot.

The groan that ripped from Elijah's throat made Alex's cock go from a semi to a Louisville Slugger.

Elijah reached a hand back and cupped Alex's neck, holding him close. "I've gotten tennis elbow from jacking off to the skyline scene we shot."

Alex chuckled, popping the button on Elijah's jeans and sliding a hand beneath the waistband and grabbing hold. God, he'd missed the feel of that hard dick in his hand. More importantly, he'd missed the man attached to it. "Lucky for you, I'm here to help."

Elijah turned in his arms and stripped the shirt off Alex's back and skirted his fingertips through the light mat of hair on his chest. "You sure this is what you want?"

"It isn't just *this*—the sex—that I want, it's *you* that I want. I'm sorry it took me so long to figure it out."

"You had a lot on the line. You coming out—"

"Had to happen. I'm not the kind of guy who could have

lived their whole professional career in the closet, hiding who I really am and, more importantly, hiding who I loved."

He'd told Elijah he loved him at the press conference, but now that they were alone, he needed to repeat it, to make sure those words sank in.

Alex sucked in a deep breath. Having pushed all of his chips to the center of the table and throwing his cards down, revealing what lived in his heart so soon into their relationship could be premature, but he couldn't hide his feelings.

Despite not wanting to live his life in the closet, he wouldn't have done what he had in front of the press if he hadn't been terrified he'd lose Elijah for good.

"I—" Elijah cut himself off. The conflict, and perhaps some deserved confusion, swirled in his eyes.

Alex didn't know if Elijah was going to say he loved him, too, but the hesitation was there. His rapid one-eighty must be a lot for Elijah to take in. Hell, he'd been happy Elijah had agreed to have dinner with him. He hadn't expected Elijah to agree to come to his apartment.

Alex pressed his lips to Elijah's, looping his fingers in Elijah's belt loops to hold him close, or to not let him escape.

Breaking the kiss, Alex said, "You don't have to say anything. I'm not trying to pressure you into saying something you're not ready for. I'm thankful you've been willing to hear me out."

"I almost didn't." Elijah glanced away as if it were something he should be embarrassed or feel bad about.

Elijah shifted, and his hard cock brushed against Alex's thigh. Alex hissed in a breath when what he'd wanted to do was throw Elijah over his shoulder and carry him to his bed.

When Elijah met Alex's eyes again, whatever Elijah had been feeling had shifted to something heated and lascivious. "But I'm glad I did."

Elijah pulled Alex in for a kiss, his tongue invading, taking, conquering. They kissed until their breathing became labored and pre-cum soaked Alex's underwear.

When they broke apart, Elijah nipped at Alex's bottom lip. "I've missed those lips, and as much as I enjoy them on mine, I can think of a much better place for them."

Agreed. Plus, he had a little surprise for Elijah. He took Elijah's hand and led him toward the bedroom. They didn't waste any time undressing. Clothes fell to the floor, and they didn't bother kicking them out of their way.

Elijah propped up a couple pillows at the head of the bed and sat against the headboard, one knee up as he slowly jacked that magnificent cock. Alex couldn't wait to have his mouth around it, but first... the surprise.

The mattress dipped as hand over hand, Alex crawled his way up Elijah's body until their hips and dicks aligned. The hand Elijah had used to stroke himself went to Alex's ass, locking Alex against him.

Alex drew his tongue up the center of Elijah's torso and skipped it across a nipple. Bracing himself on his hands, he whispered in Elijah's ear. "I'm going to suck you, and then I want you to fuck me. Are we clear?"

Elijah groaned, his hips flexing up. "Don't tease me." He pulled back far enough to see Alex's face. "Wait, you're serious."

"Yeah."

"I'm not a small guy. You can't go from nothing to having my dick in your ass. That's not how it works. You need time and stretching and—"

"What do you think I've been doing since the last time I fucked you?"

Elijah's mouth opened and closed. Alex loved that he'd rendered him speechless.

"I'm the kind of guy that does his research, and his prep work. As long as you go slow, I can take you. All of you."

"You don't have to do this." Elijah's voice dropped to that low register that made Alex's balls tight. "Anal sex isn't everything. There are plenty of amazing things we can do to get each other off."

"I know that." Then it hit Alex. Maybe Elijah wasn't into topping. "Look, if you don't want—"

Elijah chuckled. It came out deliciously dark and insanely sexy. "Oh, I want."

Elijah laced his fingers behind his head and raised his brows at Alex in a go-on-with-your-bad-self kind of way. "Don't keep me waiting," he teased.

Alex worked his way back down Elijah's body with a series of open mouth kisses, his fingers tweaking Elijah's sensitive nipples as he went. He couldn't wait to get his mouth on Elijah again. He'd woken up on more than one occasion having dreamt about blowing Elijah, of having his mouth stuffed full and tasting Elijah's cum at the back of his throat.

Settling between Elijah's legs, Alex cupped Elijah's balls and gripped his shaft. Elijah's head thunked against the headboard and his eyes closed.

Alex ran the flat of his tongue up Elijah's cock and lapped up the pre-cum. Then he took Elijah deep, relaxing the back of his throat.

"Like that, babe." Elijah's hands went to the back of Alex's head and held him there as he gently thrust upward.

The way that term of endearment rolled of Elijah's tongue engulfed him like a warm blanket being wrapped around Alex's heart. No matter what Alex's coming out did to his career, he knew his decision at the press conference had been the right one.

Baseball might come or go, but Elijah was what he needed in his life.

Alex worked Elijah with his tongue, his mouth, his hands. Fast and slow and tenacious. Elijah's fingers tangled in Alex's hair, encouraging, coaxing. Alex glanced up to see Elijah staring down at him, watching every move, every sweep of his tongue with heat and delicious, decadent intent.

Elijah's hips bucked up, and he pulled Alex off him. "You keep going and I'm going to come."

Alex sucked one of Elijah's balls into his mouth then let it fall free. The muscles in Elijah's abdomen fluttered, and his hips kicked up of their own accord.

Alex loved that he had Elijah on the ragged edge. "I thought that was the point."

"Come here." Elijah pulled Alex up to him. "I don't want to have to wait until I've recovered to have your ass. I want it now." He pressed a kiss to Alex's lips, then took it deeper, his tongue sweeping through Alex's mouth. "God, I love how I taste in your mouth."

Fuck foreplay.

He needed Elijah inside him. Now. Alex rolled onto his back and took Elijah with him. "Lube and rubbers are in the drawer."

Elijah reached across Alex, opened the nightstand drawer and pulled the needed items out. Then his hand went in again, a smile on his face when he held up the biggest of the three butt plugs from the set Alex had ordered. "I like a man who's ambitious."

"I figured it's better to be over-prepared. That way there are no surprises."

Elijah's grin sent a zing straight to Alex's groin. Alex needed to get his hands back on his man. "You need to get over here."

In a few deft moves, Elijah slid the condom down. Alex stroked himself as Elijah slicked lube all over his own girthy cock. Damn. Maybe he should have experimented with a butt plug the next size up.

Elijah settled on his knees between Alex's legs and spread a little lube on his hole. Slowly, Elijah worked one finger in, then another, stretching him wider, and working his fingers in and out. Alex groaned and slowly started fucking himself on Elijah's fingers.

Alex blew out a breath. "*Jesus Christ,* that feels good."

Elijah pressed a kiss on the inside of Alex's thigh. "You're so tight. I can't wait to fuck that ass."

Pleasure spiraled through Alex. His head fell back with a grunt as Elijah added a second finger. The butt plugs had been hot, but couldn't compare to having Elijah's fingers inside him, working him.

Elijah's hands and mouth caressed and kissed Alex's inner thigh, coming close to his cock, but always veering off, teasing and ramping Alex up higher and higher. His balls drew up. No way was he coming without Elijah inside him.

Alex reached down and forced Elijah to look at him. "Fuck me, Elijah. *Now.*"

"I promise I'll go slow. If you need me to stop—"

"The only thing I need you to stop doing right now is talking."

"Fair enough." Elijah grinned that devastating grin that made Alex's cock twitch and his lungs seize.

How did Alex get so lucky to have Elijah in his life?

Elijah settled deeper between Alex's legs, his hands going to Alex's hips, raising them higher until his cock rested against Alex's hole. Alex blew out a breath as Elijah gently thrust.

Elijah held onto Alex's hip with one hand and caressed him with the other—over Alex's inner thighs, his lower abdomen, the base of his cock, his balls. The touch pulled Alex together and at the same time tore him apart.

In and out, Elijah worked his cock until Alex completely sheathed him. "Give me a second."

Alex willed his body to relax. He'd put himself in good hands, yet he'd never felt so nakedly vulnerable.

Or so full, so... complete.

Moisture beaded on Elijah's brow and dripped down his chest, the scent of musk, sex, and sweat heavy in the air.

Elijah leaned down, devouring Alex with a kiss, their tongues dueling and tangling. "You feel so good."

Alex's reply was a slow thrust downwards that ripped a groan from Elijah. "Holy fu—*gah*."

Elijah sat back, bracing his hands on Alex's hips as he began to thrust. Alex had never been so hard. He reached down and stroked himself, mirroring Elijah's thrusts. In no time, Alex's climax built. His breathing got ragged, his balls buzzed, and he surged against Elijah, taking him fast and deep.

Alex pumped himself harder, and the world dissolved around him into flashes of light and color and sound, his ass pulsing and contracting around Elijah. Elijah grunted, his thrusts short but deep and then he, too, tumbled into bliss.

When Elijah finished, he pulled out. Alex felt relieved and bereft at the same time. Elijah disappeared long enough to dispose of the condom. He brought back a warm washcloth and wiped Alex's cum off his abdomen.

Elijah dropped the towel over the side of the bed and stretched out beside Alex, an arm draped across his waist as he pressed kisses to the ball of Alex's shoulder.

Elijah caught his breath first. "That was off the fucking charts, babe. How are you doing?"

Alex rolled onto his side to face him. "Sore, but in the best way possible." He couldn't stop looking at Elijah. At the way the sheepish grin toyed with the corners of his mouth, the way lust burned in his eyes, the way Elijah's forehead creased with his concern for Alex's wellbeing.

Elijah may not have said he loved Alex, but Elijah's love settled around him, a warm cloak in the battering winds of a winter storm.

Kissing his way up Elijah's neck, Alex said, "Thank you for giving us a second chance."

15

———

At the end of May, Elijah fought his way through the crowds of his fellow graduates and their families, searching for Alex, Trevor, and Demetri, until he came around a clump of navy-blue gowns and spotted them. For the morning graduation, Alex had decked himself out in a full suit and tie. Elijah couldn't believe he was the lucky man to call Alex his own.

His in every way but one.

And he had plans to rectify that. Today.

Alex turned and spotted Elijah, and he smiled that smile that always made Elijah's heart skip and his cock twitch. Alex scooped him up and hugged him tightly. He pressed a kiss to his neck and whispered in his ear, "I'm so damn proud of you."

Elijah hadn't heard those words often growing up, now hearing it from the man he loved bowled him over emotionally. The backs of his eyes stung, and he had to divert his focus and shake Trevor and Demetri's hands to keep from losing it.

"Congrats," they both said in turn.

"Thanks. I'm glad it's over. There were some days there where I wasn't sure I'd get through."

"Everybody has those days," Demetri said. "I never had any doubts about you, though."

"Where's your mortarboard?" Alex asked.

Elijah had his diploma in his hand, an engagement ring in a box in his pocket, and a simple question in his head. That was all that mattered.

Alex had a rare two days off in a row, and Elijah planned on taking full advantage of it starting tonight at the room they'd booked in the mountains.

"I tossed it in the air with everyone else. I have no idea where it went."

Alex opened his mouth to say something, but his phone rang. It was the ring tone for John Fogerty's *Centerfield*. The ring tone Alex had given to Coach King. Alex held up a finger and turned to walk away. "I need to take this."

The southern California sun burned through Elijah's dark graduation gown, and he stripped out of it.

"You're going to propose tonight, right?" Trevor asked.

That flutter in Elijah's stomach went off again, landing more like aftershocks from an earthquake than butterflies. "That's the plan."

"I'm still mad you didn't ask my permission for his hand," Trevor teased, "But I'll try to get over it between now and the bachelor party."

Demetri rolled his eyes.

"That's assuming he says 'yes,'" Trevor added.

Trevor wasn't helping the whole aftershocks in his stomach thing. "Anyone ever tell you that you're a douche b—"

Alex turned and put his phone away, the expression on his face unreadable. Had Alex been cut from the team? That didn't make sense, his ERA was one of the lowest of all the Double-A pitchers.

"What's wrong?" Elijah went to him, not waiting for Alex to walk back to the group.

Trevor and Demetri followed. Nervous energy wafted off Alex like a high voltage line. Eyes wide, Alex rubbed at the back of his neck.

"I've got bad news." Alex met Elijah's gaze. "I've got to leave. I can't go to the mountains with you."

Trevor and Demetri both darted glances Elijah's way. Elijah's hand slipped into his pocket, his fingers going around the velvet box. *Just because you can't ask him tonight, doesn't mean you can't ask him another night. It's all good.*

Elijah tried to tamp down on his disappointment. "But—" Elijah cut himself off, hating the desperation in his voice.

Desperation was never sane or sexy.

Whatever had happened, clearly it tore Alex up inside. This wasn't about Elijah. He cleared his throat and tried again. "What happened?"

"The Grizzlies called me up."

"*What?*" Elijah couldn't believe his ears.

Trevor whooped and clapped Alex on the back. "Way to go, man."

"Congratulations," Demetri said.

"I-I have to be at the Grizzlies' field in an hour for warm-ups. I'm starting the game."

Elijah took him by the face and planted a big wet one on his mouth. "Why are you still standing here?"

Alex held onto Elijah's wrists. "I was really looking forward to tonight. This is your special day and—"

"And now it's your special day, too. We can go to the mountains after the game and—"

Alex shook his head. What small smile he'd allowed disappeared. "I fly with the team to New York tonight for a three-game series, then off to Boston for another four."

"Go," Elijah said. "It's okay."

"Yeah?"

Elijah brought him in for another kiss, this one with a hint of tongue and a lot of promise. His man was going back to the show! Elijah grinned. "Fuck yeah."

Alex scooped Elijah up and swung him around, planting another kiss on his lips when Elijah's feet hit the ground again. "Thanks for understanding."

Trevor shooed Alex with his hands. "Go. You don't want to be late."

Alex started walking backward toward the car. "I'll leave you guys tickets at Will Call."

"Go," Trevor said again.

"We'll be there," Elijah called out as Alex started jogging to his car.

Elijah turned to Demetri, his own emotions in an uproar. This was the day Alex had worked so hard for and Elijah was thrilled, but he'd also had his heart set on asking Alex to marry him. But if he and Alex were going to have a life together, he figured he'd have to get used to the demands of Alex's job.

"I guess I'm gonna need a ride home."

"Sure thing." Demetri pulled his key fob from his pocket. "Sorry about the proposal."

Elijah only shrugged because his throat had gone tight.

Trevor fell into step beside him as they walked to the parking lot. Many of the graduates and their families had already cleared out, though some had spread out and were taking pictures. "He'll be back next week, you can—"

Trevor didn't finish his sentence, but he got this look on his face that would get a kid grounded. "I've got an idea. No promises, but I think we can make this proposal work."

We? Since when had his proposal become a group project?

"Meet me at Will Call an hour before the game, and I'll let you know if it's a go."

———

THIS WAS SUCH A BAD IDEA.

So many things could go wrong, the least of which was Alex turning down his proposal on national television.

Overall, Alex's Double-A team had been welcoming since Alex had come out, accepting Alex and Elijah as well, except for a select few. But those guys valued their jobs and feared Coach King's threat of being cut from the team too much to cause any trouble.

That Alex had produced and won games since the start of the season hadn't hurt any either. Those wins had gotten the fans on their side.

But this... this public proposal was, as they say in the profession, a whole nother ball game.

And to help pull off this impending disaster, Trevor had apparently called in a few favors.

Now, Elijah stood in the Grizzlies' bullpen with Trevor, Demetri, and the team's relievers dressed in an authentic Grizzlies' uniform. Someone with a sense of humor had given him the number sixty-nine.

The crowd noise reverberated off Elijah's eardrums all but rendering him deaf. It was the top of the sixth inning. The score tied one to one. Alex had pitched lights out, but his stamina had flagged. The other team had a runner at first, the number three batter at the plate, and the cleanup batter on deck.

No outs.

Fuck.

Alex worked a three-and-oh count up to full with two heaters high and inside. Elijah felt the trembles again, but he couldn't tell if it were really an earthquake—this was California after all—the rumble of the crowd yelling and stomping their feet, or his stomach rolling over again and again.

Alex might be taken out of the game any minute.

And then it would be Elijah's turn on the mound.

Elijah held his breath as Alex took one last glance at the runner on first and threw from the stretch. The bat connected with the ball, but the bat shattered, sending a shard toward the mound and glancing off Alex's shin.

Trevor squeezed Elijah's shoulder. "Breathe."

The ball bounced on the far side of the mound, the shortstop took it on a short hop and tossed it to the second baseman who got the out at second and fired the ball to first.

"He's out!" Trevor yelled as the Grizzlies completed a double play. Elijah could barely hear him over the roar of the crowd.

"Hot damn," Demetri said.

"Is Alex okay?"

Elijah watched Alex walk around in front of the mound with a slight limp. A trainer came out of the dugout, but Alex waved him off, telling him he was okay.

They only needed one more out. Alex walked back up to the mound to face the cleanup hitter. Then his coach called time.

The phone in the bullpen rang and the man who answered it called out to one of the relievers who'd been warming up. "You're up, Duncan."

On the JumboTron, Alex talked into his glove with his coach, shaking his head and pointing emphatically at the batter. The coach looked to the bullpen to call in the reliever. The glove fell from Alex's face, and Elijah read the emphatic *fuck* on Alex's lips.

Alex went to leave the mound, but his coach put a staying hand on his arm.

"Your turn," the bullpen coach said to Elijah. "Good luck."

Elijah swallowed hard. "Thanks, man."

"Go get him," Trevor said as he turned on the mic the sound guys had wired Elijah up with.

Did he say this was a bad idea?

The JumboTron camera had focused in on Alex. He fumed. He'd pitched fantastic, but he was being taken out of the game one out short of closing out the inning. Who's to say if they would have kept him in if the bat hadn't hit his leg.

As Elijah jogged out to the mound, he figured the bat shard had been a good excuse for the coach to take Alex out. Alex had been tiring. Alex knew it. The coach knew it. The other team knew it.

The infield had closed in around the mound. Alex had looked around and seen Elijah jogging in, but with the hat, and the uniform, and the distance, Alex apparently hadn't recognized him.

When Elijah got to the mound, the second baseman gave him a thump on the rump with the back of his glove. The rest of Alex's teammates fell away, going back to their positions. The coach took the game ball Alex had given him and handed it off to Elijah, a sly grin on his face.

It was then that Alex turned to look at Elijah as he took a step off the mound. Alex did a double take and came back. "What are you doing here?"

The mic near Elijah's collar picked up Alex's voice. The general buzz of the crowd settled as the cameras focused on them for the JumboTron feed.

Alex glanced at his team's dugout. His coach gave him a thumbs up. A few people in the crowd must have guessed what was going on because they whistled.

Here goes nothing.

Elijah pulled the velvet box out of his pocket and went down on one knee. The intermittent whistles echoed around the stadium.

"Alex..." Elijah's voice filled the air. The crowd went silent. The staccato beat of his heart thumping so hard in his chest it would leave a bruise. "I love you."

Alex dropped his glove, and his hand went up and swiped off his cap. He shook his head. Elijah didn't know if that meant Alex didn't want to hear what Elijah had to say or if he couldn't believe Elijah was going to say it.

But Elijah wouldn't let a minor thing like the possibility of national humiliation stop him.

"I love you. I don't know where the crazy train we're on is going or where it will stop next, I only know that I want to ride it with you." Elijah held out the simple platinum band. "Will you marry me?"

For a second, Alex didn't move, but Elijah saw his chest hitch and his eyes blink back the moisture gathering there. Then Alex nodded, almost imperceptibly.

"Yes?"

Alex took Elijah's hand and pulled him to his feet, then leaned into the microphone and said, "Yes. I'll marry you."

The JumboTron burst with electronic fireworks, the words 'yes, yes, yes' blinking and twinkling across the screen. From the noise from the crowd, you'd have thought the Grizzlies had just won the World Series.

I guess everyone was a sucker for a proposal.

Then Alex pulled Elijah in tight, and in front of forty-three thousand spectators, and millions of network viewers, kissed him.

It was all heart, and soul, and delighted disbelief.

Then Alex covered the microphone and hollered into Elijah's ear, "I can't fucking believe you're mine."

IF YOU ENJOYED ONE SHOT, PLEASE CONSIDER LEAVING A REVIEW at GoodReads, BookBub, or your favorite retailer. Reviews are always much appreciated!

TURN THE PAGE FOR MORE OF BLACK STALLION STUDIOS

A LETTER TO MY READERS

Dear Reader,

Never fear, the lights are always on at Black Stallion Studios. And now it's time the spotlight shifted…

For Grant Hardy, the closet is a lonely place. And it's about time the straight-acting stud got out of gay p*rn.

But a betrayal forces him to keep working to save his grandmother's home.

And that secret affair he's having with Sebastian? Isn't so secret anymore. Now everything he's worked his ass off for is at stake.

Can he f*ck his way into solvency?

Will the truth set him free to love the man he wants?

Or will his family suffer the consequences?

Key Grip is a steamy, sexy romp on the wild side you can't miss.

Get it here: https://books2read.com/KeyGrip

Lazy S Ranch Series
Romantic Suspense

Cowgirl, Unexpectedly (Lazy S Ranch 1)
Must Love Horses (Lazy S Ranch 2)
Hot on the Trail (Lazy S Ranch 3)
Cowboy, Undercover (Lazy S Ranch 4)
Cowboy, Unbridled (Lazy S Ranch 5)
Cowgirl, Unbroken (Lazy S Ranch 6)

Rockin' Rodeo Series
Contemporary Romance

Luck of the Draw (Rockin' Rodeo 1)
Photo Chute (Rockin' Rodeo 2)
Reined In (Rockin' Rodeo 3)
Rockin' Rodeo Series Collection Books 1-3

Wright's Island Series
Romantic Suspense

Don't Look Back (Wright's Island 1)
In Her Defense (Wright's Island 2)

Black Stallion Studios Series
MM Romance

One Shot (Book 1)
Key Grip (Book 2)
Best Boy (Book 3)

ABOUT THE AUTHOR

Vicki Tharp makes her home on small acreage in south Texas with her husband and an embarrassing number of pets. When she isn't writing, you can usually find her on the back of her horse—avoiding anything that remotely resembles housework —smelling like fly spray and horse sweat.

Join my newsletter at: http://eepurl.com/croJgz
Join my street team and receive free Advance Reader Copies of my upcoming books at: http://eepurl.com/cWhXbD
You can find my website at: www.VickiTharp.com
I love to hear from readers. You can email me at vwtharp@VickiTharp.com

Or you can stalk me at:

facebook.com/VickiTharpAuthor

instagram.com/author_Vicki_Tharp

bookbub.com/authors/vicki-tharp

amazon.com/author/vicki_tharp

twitter.com/vwtharp

www.ingramcontent.com/pod-product-compliance
Lightning Source LLC
Chambersburg PA
CBHW050528190726
48284CB00003B/986